PINE BOX PAYOFF

In a voice tight with suppressed anger, Stoddard asked, "Are you going to work for me or not?"

"Not hardly," Fargo said. "I've still got over eighty dollars of your money. I'll send it over to the hotel tomorrow. I spent the rest on supplies getting here."

"Don't bother," Stoddard snapped. All pretense of geniality had vanished. "You should keep it. You never know—you might need to pay for a funeral someday."

He didn't have to say the rest of what he meant. Fargo understood it just fine.

You'll die next!

THE TRAILSMAN

#309

CALIFORNIA CARNAGE

by

Jon Sharpe

A SIGNET BOOK

SIGNET
Published by New American Library, a division of
Penguin Group (USA) Inc., 375 Hudson Street,
New York, New York 10014, USA
Penguin Group (Canada), 90 Eglinton Avenue East, Suite 700, Toronto,
Ontario M4P 2Y3, Canada (a division of Pearson Penguin Canada Inc.)
Penguin Books Ltd., 80 Strand, London WC2R 0RL, England
Penguin Ireland, 25 St. Stephen's Green, Dublin 2,
Ireland (a division of Penguin Books Ltd.)
Penguin Group (Australia), 250 Camberwell Road, Camberwell, Victoria 3124,
Australia (a division of Pearson Australia Group Pty. Ltd.)
Penguin Books India Pvt. Ltd., 11 Community Centre, Panchsheel Park,
New Delhi - 110 017, India
Penguin Group (NZ), 67 Apollo Drive, Rosedale, North Shore,
Auckland 0745, New Zealand (a division of Pearson New Zealand Ltd.)
Penguin Books (South Africa) (Pty.) Ltd., 24 Sturdee Avenue,
Rosebank, Johannesburg 2196, South Africa

Penguin Books Ltd., Registered Offices:
80 Strand, London WC2R 0RL, England

First published by Signet, an imprint of New American Library,
a division of Penguin Group (USA) Inc.

First Printing, July 2007
10 9 8 7 6 5 4 3 2 1

The first chapter of this book previously appeared in *Border Bravados,* the
three hundred eighth volume in this series.

Copyright © Penguin Group (USA) Inc., 2007
All rights reserved

Ⓟ REGISTERED TRADEMARK—MARCA REGISTRADA

Printed in the United States of America

The Trailsman

Beginnings . . . they bend the tree and they mark the man. Skye Fargo was born when he was eighteen. Terror was his midwife, vengeance his first cry. Killing spawned Skye Fargo, ruthless, cold-blooded murder. Out of the acrid smoke of gunpowder still hanging in the air, he rose, cried out a promise never forgotten.

The Trailsman they began to call him all across the West: searcher, scout, hunter, the man who could see where others only looked, his skills for hire but not his soul, the man who lived each day to the fullest, yet trailed each tomorrow. Skye Fargo, the Trailsman, the seeker who could take the wildness of a land and the wanting of a woman and make them his own.

California, 1858—
where the stagecoaches that run
along the Old Mission Trail
carry trouble for the Trailsman.

1

The swift patter of footsteps along the street told the big man in buckskins that something was wrong. He stood in the shadows of an alley mouth with his lake blue eyes narrowed, waiting to see what was going to happen.

The girl came out of the night. Her long brown hair whipped around her shoulders as she jerked her head back and forth to look for any sign of her pursuers. She was on the far side of the street from the man in the shadows, but he could see her fairly well in the light that spilled through the doorways of several cantinas, still open at this late hour.

From somewhere in the darkness, a man stepped out in front of the fleeing girl. She skidded to an abrupt halt and cast wild glances around her, looking for somewhere else to run.

Before she could move, the man came toward her, his arms outstretched. She opened her mouth to scream. It was a hot, muggy night in the pueblo of Los Angeles, a night for screaming.

But before she could make a sound, the man clapped a rough hand over her mouth and grabbed her arm with his other hand. Cruel fingers dug into the flesh.

"I've got the bitch," he called to whoever had been pursuing the girl. Their hurried steps came closer.

Across the street, Skye Fargo strode out of the shadows and said, "Let her go."

His voice was deep and powerful; it carried well even though he didn't raise it. The man holding the girl rasped a curse and swung around, pulling her with him so that she was between him and Fargo.

"Who the hell—"

"I said, let her go," Fargo repeated as he continued across the street in an unhurried fashion. He was a muscular man, a little above medium height, bigger than he appeared to be at first glance, with the speed and power of a wolf rather than the bulk of a bull. A short, dark beard sprouted on his jaw, and intelligent eyes peered out from under the broad brim of a sand-colored hat.

"What business is it of yours?" the man who held the girl challenged. "Better light a shuck out of here, hombre, before you wind up in trouble."

A faint smile touched Fargo's lips. "I don't think I'm all that worried by threats from a low-down skunk who manhandles girls."

"You son of a bitch. You don't know who this little bitch is—"

At that moment, the girl sank her teeth into the palm of the hand over her mouth.

The man screeched in pain, jerked his hand away, and hauled her around so that she faced him. Blood covered the palm of the hand she had bitten as he raised it to smash her face.

The blow didn't land because Fargo had never stopped moving, and a couple of quick steps brought him in reach while the man was pulling his arm back to strike. Fargo's right fist shot out in a short, sharp punch that smashed into the man's face. The man let

2

go of the girl as he stumbled backward. He caught his balance and clawed at the butt of the gun stuck behind his belt.

Fargo didn't give him a chance to pull the weapon. He bored in, fast and hard, sinking a left in the man's belly. Whiskey-laden breath gusted out of the man's mouth. Fargo threw a right cross that clipped the man on the chin, and followed it with a looping left that landed with a solid impact on the jaw. The man went to his knees and then toppled onto his side. He lay there gasping for breath and groaning in a soft voice.

Fargo stepped back and turned as he heard a rush of footsteps behind him. The man's friends had caught up.

The Colt in Fargo's hand rose as he came around to face the others. They stopped short as they saw the black mouth of the gun's muzzle pointing at them. The heavy revolver was rock steady.

"Move over here behind me," he told the girl, who was staring at the man Fargo had knocked down. She did as he said, scurrying to put him between her and the men who had been chasing her.

Three men glared at Fargo in the dim light. Like their friend, they were roughly dressed, beard-stubbled hardcases, the sort of no-accounts who could be found in the saloons and whorehouses of any frontier town. One of them demanded, "What the hell did you do to Elam?"

Another of the men said, "Better put that gun down, mister, before somebody gets hurt."

"It'll be you who does," Fargo said.

"Damn it, there's three of us and one of you, and we're armed, too!"

"That means I'll kill two before any of you get off a shot. The third man *might* be able to hit me, but I'll kill him, too, before I go down."

From the grim, worried looks on their faces, none of them doubted what Fargo said.

"Hell, take the little slut, and good riddance," one of the men said. "We don't want her that bad. And after you've been saddled with her for a while, you won't, either. She's nothin' but trouble."

Fargo heard the angry hiss of the girl's indrawn breath behind him, but he didn't look around, didn't take his attention off the men he held at bay with his Colt. "I'll take my chances," he said. "Now pick up your friend and get out of here."

"You're gonna be damn sorry you ever laid eyes on us, mister."

"Too late. I already am."

Fargo moved back to give them some room as they came forward to help the first man onto his feet. He was groggy but conscious enough to stand under his own power once they got him upright. He glared at Fargo and might have tried to attack him again if one of his friends hadn't pulled on his sleeve and said, "Let's go, Elam. It's over."

"No, it ain't," Elam rumbled. "It ain't hardly over."

But he left anyway, moving off in an unsteady walk, accompanied by the other three men. Fargo didn't lower his gun until they had disappeared in the darkness down the street, and even then he didn't holster the weapon.

"Mister, I can't thank you enough—" the girl began.

Fargo turned to her and grasped her arm with his free hand. His touch was gentle compared to that of the man who had grabbed her before. His voice held a note of urgency, though, as he said, "I don't trust those varmints. Let's get off the street before they double back and try to bushwhack us."

She gasped. "You think they would?"

"They might." Fargo steered her toward one of the

nearby cantinas. "We'll be safe enough in there, where it's light."

He had at least one friend there, too, because the place was run by a man named Pablo Almendovar, whose life had been saved by Fargo several years earlier. In fact, Fargo had been headed for Pablo's cantina when he'd heard the hurrying footsteps and his instincts told him trouble was about to emerge from the darkness.

He'd been right about that. Over the long, eventful years he had learned to trust his instincts, and they had seldom betrayed him.

The atmosphere inside the cantina was close and smoky despite the open door. Not much air stirred tonight. Half a dozen men stood at the bar, drinking, while another half dozen were scattered at the rough tables. In one corner, an old man strummed a guitar. His blind eyes gazed out at the room, and what they saw, only he knew.

The massive man behind the bar had a wild tangle of black hair and a jutting beard. His dark eyes lit up as he noticed Fargo. "Skye! Welcome, *mi amigo*, welcome!" His gaze moved to the girl beside Fargo, and his bushy eyebrows rose in appreciation.

Fargo holstered his gun and headed for one of the empty tables, signaling to Pablo to bring drinks. He held a chair for the girl, then sat down opposite her. In the smoky light from the cantina's lamps, he saw that she was older than he had taken her for, around twenty years old, more of a young woman than a girl.

And although she was dressed in a long, colorfully embroidered skirt and a low-cut, short-sleeved white blouse that left her shoulders bare, the sort of outfit that the Mexican girls here in Los Angeles wore, she was not Mexican. Her clothes and her long dark hair had made her appear otherwise in the dim light outside.

5

But her eyes were light blue and her skin was fair and creamy. Her heritage might be pure Spanish, but there was no indio blood in her. Fargo wondered if she belonged to one of the old Californio families, the Spaniards who had ruled California before it became part of the United States ten years earlier.

"Thank you," she said in unaccented English. "I don't know what would have happened if you hadn't helped me."

"Nothing good, I'd wager," Fargo said. "I reckon introductions are in order. My name is Skye Fargo."

"I'm Belinda Grayson," she introduced herself. Not Spanish at all. She frowned and went on. "Your name seems familiar, Mr. Fargo. I believe my father may have mentioned you. Do you know him? Arthur Grayson?"

Fargo shook his head. "Afraid not." He didn't mention that he was well-known in some circles west of the Mississippi. He wouldn't be surprised if Belinda's father had heard of him.

Pablo brought mugs of coffee flavored with dark chocolate over to the table and set them in front of Fargo and Belinda. "I did not know you were visiting our humble pueblo, Skye," the burly proprietor of the cantina said. "But as always, I am glad to see you."

"The feeling's mutual, Pablo," Fargo told him. "How's Juanita?"

Pablo grinned and made a rounded motion over his belly, indicating that his wife was with child again.

Fargo chuckled. "How many does this make?"

"This will be the eighth little *niño*," Pablo said with pride in his voice. He grew more serious as he went on. "You are here on business?"

Fargo nodded. "I'm supposed to meet a man named Stoddard."

Across the table, Belinda had been sipping her coffee. But at Fargo's mention of the name, she gasped and said, "You know Hiram Stoddard?"

"Never laid eyes on the man," Fargo answered. "Why? Is there something wrong with him?"

"Those men who were after me outside . . . they work for Stoddard."

Fargo's eyes narrowed as he looked at her. He knew she was telling the truth. She was too surprised to be lying.

"Why are you supposed to meet him?" she went on.

"Some men would say that's none of your business, Miss Grayson."

Pablo withdrew to the bar with a worried frown on his face. He must have sensed the sudden tension at the table, and he didn't like it.

"I don't mean to be impolite," Belinda said. "It's just that you helped me—"

"I would have helped any woman who was in trouble," Fargo said.

"And my father and Mr. Stoddard are enemies," she continued as if she hadn't heard him. "That's why those men were after me. I'm sure of it. They were going to capture me and hold me hostage until my father agreed to give up the plans for his stagecoach line."

Fargo began to have a glimmering of what was going on. He had thought that the men were after Belinda simply because she was a pretty girl and they wanted to have some fun with her. Their actions could have been motivated by more than that, though.

"Your father and Stoddard are both trying to establish stagecoach lines that will follow the Old Mission Trail along the coast to northern California," Fargo guessed.

Belinda nodded. "That's right. They've clashed before, in other places, over other business deals." She sighed. "They're mortal enemies, I suppose you could say. But my father is an honorable man, while Mr. Stoddard would stop at nothing to get what he wants."

That was the way she saw it, anyway, Fargo thought. The story might be very different if Stoddard were the one telling it.

On the other hand, the man called Elam had treated Belinda roughly, and Fargo had no doubt that the other three would have, too. They had looked like the sorts who wouldn't draw the line at abusing a woman.

If Stoddard had varmints like that working for him, then Fargo didn't have a very high opinion of the man. He figured that, in all likelihood, he wouldn't want to take any job Stoddard offered him.

But along with a letter, Stoddard had sent him a hundred dollars to come here to Los Angeles and meet with him to discuss employment, and Fargo had taken the money. He would have to talk to Stoddard face-to-face and then make up his mind what he was going to do. If he didn't accept Stoddard's proposal, he would return what was left of the hundred bucks. That was the only fair way to handle things.

Meanwhile, he asked Belinda, "Are you sure those hombres weren't after you for . . . other reasons?"

She blushed, and her face was even prettier as the warm pink tinge crept across it. "I suppose that's possible," she admitted. "But they know who I am, and I just don't believe it was their idea to come after me. I think Mr. Stoddard sent them."

"What were you doing on the street at this time of night?"

At that blunt question, her chin came up with a hint of defiance and stubbornness. "I'm accustomed to walking where I please, when I please."

"Maybe so," Fargo said, "but out here on the frontier that can be dangerous. We're not back wherever it is you come from."

"I assure you, there are dangers there, too."

Fargo didn't doubt it. But he hadn't gotten an answer to his question, either, so he continued giving her a steady stare as he waited.

"I was just trying to get a breath of fresh air," she said after a moment. "My hotel room was stifling."

His nod encompassed the clothes she wore. "What's with the getup?"

"The way these Spanish and Mexican girls dress is very comfortable," Belinda said. "I bought these clothes at the market the other day and wanted to try them. Besides, they look good, don't you think?"

Fargo thought they looked very good indeed. The shoulders left bare by the blouse were smooth, inviting a man's touch. And the neckline of the garment was low enough so that the twin swells of her firm young breasts showed above it, along with the upper part of the dark valley between them. That cleft made a man think about what it would feel like to put his face in it and run his tongue over her heated skin.

"You look good enough that I'd better walk you back to your hotel," Fargo said, "just so nobody else who's out and about tonight will be tempted."

She smiled and asked, "What about you, Mr. Fargo? Are you tempted?"

She was a natural-born flirt, he thought, and she had read what was in his mind without any trouble at all. He growled, "I've had saddles older than you."

Hurt by the words, she blinked her eyes and frowned at him.

He drank the last of his coffee and got to his feet. "Come on."

"Maybe I don't want to go with you," she said.

"You'd be a fool not to. Up to you."

She glanced through the cantina's open doorway at the dark night outside, and he saw the irritation she felt toward him warring with her nervousness. The nervousness won.

"All right," she said as she stood up.

As they walked out, Fargo called to Pablo, "I'll be back later, amigo."

"A room will be waiting for you when you return, Skye," Pablo promised.

Fargo and Belinda walked down the street without touching. Los Angeles was a small pueblo, but it was growing. In the eight years since California had become a state, quite a few Anglo settlers had moved in to join the Spanish and Mexican citizens who had populated the place since the founding of Mission San Gabriel, just east of the pueblo that had grown up nearby. The buildings had all been made of adobe at first, but now there were a fair number of frame structures, including the two-story hotel where Belinda and her father were staying.

That was the same hotel where Fargo was supposed to meet Hiram Stoddard, he noted. He supposed the enmity between Stoddard and Grayson didn't keep them from staying in the same hostelry, especially since it was the most comfortable lodging in town.

Fargo and Belinda went up the three steps to the porch that ran along the front of the hotel. He paused and said, "I reckon you'll be all right now."

"Aren't you coming in?" she asked. "Mr. Stoddard is staying here, I believe."

"I'll talk to him later. Right now I want to tend to my horse." He had left the magnificent black-and-white Ovaro stallion tied at a hitch rail down the street, not far from the cantina. Pablo had a stable and a corral out back where pilgrims who rented the rooms in the rear of the cantina could leave their

10

mounts. Fargo intended to see to it that the Ovaro was unsaddled, rubbed down, and given grain and water before he dealt with the rest of the business that had brought him to Los Angeles.

"All right. Thank you again, Mr. Fargo."

He tugged on the brim of his hat. "You're welcome, Miss Grayson. Good night."

She went inside the hotel. Fargo waited until she had closed the door behind her before he turned away.

Across the street, Colt flame bloomed in the darkness, and Fargo heard the wind rip of a bullet as it tore through the air next to his ear.

2

As the slug splintered wood somewhere behind him, Fargo threw himself to the right, lunging off the porch so that the light through the hotel's front windows wouldn't make him a better target. By the time his boots hit the dirt of the street, his gun was in his hand.

More muzzle flashes gouted from the shadows across the street. Fargo ducked behind a two-wheeled mule cart that someone had left there after unhitching the mule. It didn't provide much cover but was better than nothing.

Lead came out of the night, searching for him, thudding into the cart. He crouched low, thrust his Colt around the corner of the cart, and triggered three fast shots toward the dark alley mouth where the gunmen lurked. Someone yelled in pain, telling Fargo that he had winged one of them, at the least.

They spilled from the alley: dark, running figures that split up, two going right, two going left. They wanted to circle around him, get him in a cross fire. Fargo knew that as well as he knew his own name.

He couldn't afford to let that happen, so he tracked the men sprinting to the right and fired the two rounds he had remaining in the Colt's cylinder. Hitting a running man in bad light was no easy task, but one of the bushwhackers yelped and tumbled off his feet. He rolled over a couple of times and then lay still.

But the other one kept running and ducked behind a water trough.

Fargo bit back a curse as he started to reload. Now he would have them coming at him from two sides. If they had done that to start with, they probably would have gotten him with their first volley. They had over-estimated their gun skill, though, all four of them opening up at him from the alley across the street.

Fargo's eyes were sharper than those of most men, but even he couldn't see in the dark. He glanced to the left and saw no sign of the men who had gone that way. They were hiding somewhere in the shadows. He would have to rely on his other senses to warn him of their approach. As he finished reloading the Colt, putting six in the wheel this time instead of the cus-tomary five, he kept his eyes on the water trough where the third man had taken cover.

A flurry of shots came from Fargo's left, chipping away at the framework of the cart. No doubt thinking that Fargo would be distracted by that, the man be-hind the water trough leaped up and tried to dash across the street, so he would be on the same side as his quarry.

Fargo ignored the other threat for the moment, lined his sights on the running man, and squeezed the trigger. As the Colt roared, the man went backward as if he had been punched in the chest by a giant fist.

As soon as Fargo saw the man start to go down and knew he had scored a clean hit, he twisted around and flattened himself on the ground. The other two men had reached the boardwalk on this side of the street and now charged toward him, the guns in their fists spewing lead. Fargo took aim and fired three times, fast.

One of the attackers spun around and staggered into the street like he was doing a crazy dance. The other man stumbled but stayed on his feet, lurching to the side and disappearing. Fargo figured he had ducked into a recessed doorway, or even a narrow space between buildings.

The man in the street jerked the trigger of his gun again, but the barrel pointed down now. The bullet thudded into the dirt in front of him. He dropped the gun, clutched at his midsection, then doubled over and collapsed.

That made three men lying in the street with Fargo's lead in them. He didn't know where the fourth man had gone, but no more shots rang out.

Curious yells sounded, though, as several men appeared on the street and hurried toward the hotel to see what all the shooting was about. Men came out of the hotel, too, and as Fargo glanced in that direction, he thought he caught a glimpse of Belinda Grayson casting a worried look through the front window. She had to be wondering if the shots had been directed at him.

A man hurried up, swinging a lantern in one hand. In the other he carried a shotgun. Fargo got to his feet and holstered the Colt, not wanting the fellow with the Greener to get trigger-happy.

"Hold it right there!" the man shouted at Fargo. "Don't move, damn it!"

"I don't intend to, Sheriff," Fargo said as he stood with his hands in plain sight.

"It's Marshal," the heavyset man said as he puffed to a halt in front of Fargo. The light from the hotel reflected off the badge pinned to his vest. Fargo had seen that reflection and guessed the man was the local law. "What the hell's goin' on here? Are those bodies in the street?"

"Bushwhackers," Fargo said. "They laid for me over there in that alley and opened fire as I stood on the hotel porch."

The marshal stared at him. "And you downed all three of them?" He sounded as if he had a hard time believing that.

"There were four of them. One got away."

The lawman rubbed at his jaw as he thought about that. After a moment he said, "Better give me your gun."

"I'd just as soon I didn't," Fargo said. "Like I told you, one of those bushwhackers got away. He might come back."

"Not with me here," the marshal blustered. "Now gimme that gun."

Fargo wasn't prepared to fight the lawman over it. He shrugged, slid the Colt from leather, and extended it butt-first to the marshal, who took it and stuck it behind the belt that encircled his ample waist.

"Now we'll take a look at them hombres," the marshal declared. He glanced at the men who had gathered in the street. "Ed, Tom, I'm deputizin' you. You'll help me in case any more trouble breaks out."

The two townsmen didn't look too happy about having that responsibility thrust upon them, but they nodded.

"Larch, you go fetch the undertaker," the sheriff went on to another man. "Tell him he'll have plenty o' work to do this evenin'."

"How do you know those gents are dead, Marshal?" the man he had just spoken to wanted to know.

The lawman looked at Fargo and narrowed his eyes. "Because I recognize this hombre who shot 'em," he said.

The marshal carried the lantern over to the nearest of the bodies and raised it so that the yellow glow washed over the corpse. Sightless eyes stared upward. The face was familiar to Fargo. He wasn't surprised that he recognized the man.

"You know him?" the marshal asked.

"Yeah. I don't know his name, but I was told that he works for an hombre named Stoddard. I had a run-in with him and three other men just a little while ago."

"You reckon them other two are part of the same bunch?"

"I'd bet on it," Fargo said.

His hunch turned out to be correct. He recognized the other bodies when the marshal checked on them. They were just as dead as the first one.

The only one missing was the man called Elam. Fargo was confident that he had wounded Elam, too, but not badly enough to keep him from running off.

"Wait just a minute," the lawman told him, then walked over to talk to some of the men who had come out of the hotel. Fargo waited, suppressing a feeling of impatience as he did so. A few moments later, the marshal came back to join him.

"Here you go, Fargo," the marshal said as he held out the Colt. "Since there's three bodies, and since those fellas who were in the hotel lobby said there was a bunch of shots from across the street first, it's pretty obvious you're tellin' the truth about bein' ambushed. Clear-cut case o' self-defense if you ask me, but there'll have to be an inquest anyway so a judge can say so."

Fargo took the gun and slipped it into its holster. "When?"

"The inquest, you mean? Tomorrow, I reckon. Have to get things squared away in a hurry in heat like this, so the carcasses can be planted as soon as possible. You weren't plannin' on leavin' town tonight, were you?"

Fargo glanced at the hotel. Somewhere in there were Hiram Stoddard, Arthur Grayson, and Grayson's daughter, Belinda. He had questions for all of them.

Getting shot at always made him curious.

He shook his head and told the marshal, "No, I'm not going anywhere."

Pablo looked relieved when Fargo walked into the cantina a short time later.

"I heard all the shooting up the street and knew you must have been in the middle of it, amigo," he said. "Anytime there is trouble, it seems to find you."

"On a pretty regular basis," Fargo agreed. "But I came out of this fracas without a scratch."

Pablo made the sign of the cross. "I thank the Blessed Virgin for that. I had a room made up for you. You are ready to turn in?"

Fargo shook his head. "No, I still have things to do. I put my horse out back in the stable. Thought I'd get a drink before I headed over to the hotel again."

"Another cup of coffee?"

Fargo smiled and shook his head. "Tequila."

The blind guitar player in the corner heard him, tapped his fingers on the instrument in a fast, catchy rhythm, tipped his head back, and drawing out the word said, "Tequila." A smile wreathed his seamed face.

Fargo slid a coin across the bar and tipped his head toward the old man. "Give him what he wants, on me," he told Pablo.

"I never charge the old one, anyway," Pablo replied. "He tells me it would be bad luck to do so, and who am I to argue with one who has lived so many years without sight? He must know what he is talking about, no?"

Pablo poured the drinks and took one of them over to the blind man. Fargo tossed back the fiery liquor and felt it fortify him. Pablo returned and asked, "Another?"

Fargo shook his head. "No, I have to get to that business I mentioned."

"If the cantina is closed when you return, come in the back. You have your usual room."

"Sofia won't be there waiting for me, will she?" Fargo asked with a slight frown.

"Ah, this I cannot answer for certain, amigo. You know that one. She has a mind of her own."

Fargo knew Sofia, all right. She sometimes worked as a serving girl for Pablo, and had taken a shine to Fargo when she was fourteen. She had been throwing herself at him since then, every time he came to Los Angeles and paid a visit to the cantina.

He hadn't seen her tonight, and when he counted up the years in his head and realized that she was nineteen now, he hoped that she had forgotten all about her crush on him.

But judging by what Pablo had just said, that wasn't the case. "She's still around, eh?" Fargo said.

"Very much so. And still very much in love with you, Skye. Young men pursue her, but she will have nothing to do with them."

Fargo's frown deepened. "Don't tell her I'm here, all right?"

"Of course. Whatever you wish, amigo. But if I know that one, she has already heard that you are in Los Angeles."

Fargo left the cantina and told himself to worry about Sofia later. Right now he had to deal with Hiram Stoddard and settle things with the man.

The street was quiet as Fargo approached the hotel. The guests who had been drawn out by the shooting had all gone back inside, and the townspeople had returned to their homes.

He kept a watchful eye out anyway. He didn't think Elam would make another try for him tonight, since he was sure the man was wounded, but Fargo hadn't lived as long as he had by giving too much weight to unfounded assumptions.

No one bothered him. He went inside and crossed the lobby to approach the desk.

"Hiram Stoddard," he said to the clerk on the other side of the counter.

"Is Mr. Stoddard expecting you, sir?"

Fargo nodded. "He is."

"In that case, you can go right on up. Mr. Stoddard is in room seven. Top of the stairs and down the hall to the left." The clerk added, "It's our best room, you know."

Fargo didn't care about that. He climbed the stairs and found room seven. When he knocked on the door, a voice from inside the room asked, "Who is it?"

"Skye Fargo."

Footsteps approached the door quickly, then stopped and paused as if the man didn't want to appear too eager. When the door swung back a few seconds later, the man inside greeted Fargo in a solemn voice.

"Please, come in, sir. I've been expecting you, but I didn't know exactly when you would arrive in Los Angeles."

"Just rode in this evening," Fargo said as he stepped into the room. He took his hat off and held it in his left hand, keeping his right free in case he needed to reach for his gun. Like being careful, that was another habit of his.

Hiram Stoddard closed the door. He was a tall man, a few inches taller than Fargo, with the beginnings of a paunch and a hairline that had receded nearly all the way to the back of his head. Side-whiskers bushed out on his cheeks as if trying to make up for the lack of hair on top of his head. Gold-framed spectacles perched on the bridge of his nose.

Stoddard wore a swallowtail coat and a fancy vest over a white shirt. A diamond stickpin held his cravat in place. His clothes were brushed free of dust and his boots had been shined. Despite the expensive clothes he had a certain seedy air about him, as if he would have been at home in the finest drawing rooms in New York or San Francisco, but the other people there would have looked down on him a little.

And that would annoy the hell out of him.

"Would you like a drink, Mr. Fargo?" Stoddard asked as he moved toward a sideboard. As the clerk had said, the room was large and well furnished, with a four-poster bed, a nice rug on the floor, and not one but two brass spittoons in opposite corners, so nobody staying here would ever have to go very far to spit. Stoddard went on. "I have some excellent brandy."

"No, thanks," Fargo said. "I think we should get on with our business."

"A man who gets right to the point, eh? I like that. And I would have expected as much, given the reputation you have, Mr. Fargo. What is it they call you? The Trailsman?"

Fargo nodded. "Some do."

"Because there's no one better at tracking, scouting, or laying out a new trail, or at least so I'm told. That's exactly the sort of man I need to help me in my latest venture."

"Which is?" Fargo asked, even though he had

guessed the answer while he was talking to Belinda Grayson.

"A stagecoach line that will run from here in Los Angeles all the way up to San Francisco, Mr. Fargo. California needs transportation. It's growing by leaps and bounds, and it's only going to continue to do so. I'm not talking about the sort of riffraff that flocked out here when gold was discovered, either. I'm talking about solid citizens, businessmen, and entrepreneurs, the sort of men who will make California the greatest state in the nation!"

Stoddard sounded like he was running for office. That didn't make Fargo like him any better.

"What do you want me to do?"

Stoddard raised his eyebrows. "I should have thought that was obvious. I want to hire you to lay out the route for this stage line, Mr. Fargo. I intend for it to follow the general route of the Old Mission Trail, but of course there'll be some variations, some places where it would be better to deviate from the old path. I know that with you in charge of determining the route, it will be the fastest, easiest way to get from here to San Francisco."

"You know a man named Elam?"

The blunt question appeared to take Stoddard by surprise, but he answered it after only a second's hesitation. "Yes, a man named Elam works for me."

"Doing what?"

"Bodyguard, driver, general assistant." Stoddard shrugged. "Whatever I need him to do, really."

"Does that include trying to kill me?"

Stoddard opened and closed his mouth a couple of times, but no sound came out. He reminded Fargo of a fish. If he was putting on an act, he was mighty good at it.

"I assure you, Mr. Fargo," he said at last, "I have no idea what you're talking about."

"Elam have some friends? Three hombres of the same sort he is?"

"Yes, their names are Dawlish, Barnes, and Whitney. They work for me, too."

"They did," Fargo said. "They're dead now, and I reckon Elam's got at least one bullet hole in him."

Stoddard stared at him, clearly at a loss for words.

"What about Arthur Grayson and his daughter, Belinda?" Fargo said. "You know them, too?"

Stoddard did, and the angry flush that appeared on his face told Fargo he didn't like them. "I don't know who you've been talking to," he said, "but I can assure you that anything you were told by Arthur Grayson is a lie. The man is a thief, and his hatred for me knows no bounds."

"Maybe so, but it was *your* men who tried to grab Miss Grayson off the street a little while ago."

Stoddard gave a vehement shake of his head. "I know nothing about that, sir. Nothing!"

He was a little *too* vehement about his denial this time, Fargo decided. He didn't believe Stoddard now. The man might not have known about Fargo's shootout with Elam and the others—he must have heard the shots but hadn't been out of his room to see what they were about—but he knew about what had almost happened to Belinda.

She had been right. Stoddard had sent Elam and the others after her, hoping to use her to put pressure on her father.

"Mr. Fargo, I'm confused," Stoddard went on when Fargo didn't say anything. "I don't know what's happened tonight, but I assure you I had nothing to do with it. If any of the men working for me have done anything improper, I give you my word I'll deal with them."

"A mite late for Dawlish, Barnes, and Whitney. Like I said, they're dead. But I'm sure the undertaker would be happy to let you pay for their funerals."

Stoddard wasn't very tanned to start with, and he went paler at Fargo's words. In a voice tight with suppressed anger, he asked, "Are you going to work for me or not?"

"Not hardly," Fargo said. "I've still got over eighty dollars of your money. I'll send it over to the hotel tomorrow. I spent the rest on supplies getting here."

"Don't bother," Stoddard snapped. All pretense of geniality had vanished from his bearing. "You should keep it. You never know—you might need to pay for a funeral someday."

He didn't have to say the rest of what he meant. Fargo understood it just fine.

You'll die next!

3

Fargo put his hat on and got out of there before he lost his temper and threw a punch at the son of a bitch. He went down to the lobby and asked the clerk, "How about Mr. Arthur Grayson?"

The man looked a little surprised at the question. Fargo supposed that since he had asked for Stoddard earlier, the clerk thought he wouldn't have anything to do with the Graysons.

"They're in rooms eighteen and twenty, down at the other end of the hall. Adjoining rooms, you know."

Fargo nodded and said, "Much obliged." He headed up the stairs again.

When he reached the landing, he glanced toward Stoddard's room again. The door was still closed. Stoddard would be in there thinking up ways to get what he wanted, to get back at Fargo for defying him. He was that sort of man, so full of pride that he couldn't tolerate being challenged.

Fargo hadn't thought to ask which Grayson was in which room. Since he came to eighteen first, he knocked on that door. Light footsteps sounded on the other side, and Belinda's voice asked, "Who's there, please?"

"Skye Fargo."

The door opened. She peered out at him with a frown that didn't make her any less pretty. "What are you doing here, Mr. Fargo?"

She had changed from the long skirt and peasant blouse, and now wore a silk robe belted around her trim waist. It clung to the sleek lines of her body. Fargo couldn't help but notice that, but it wasn't why he had knocked on her door.

"I was looking for your father," he told her. "Didn't know which room he was in."

"He's next door." Belinda's frown didn't go away. "If you don't mind my asking, what do you want with him?"

"I've talked to Stoddard," he said. "I won't be working for him. And you were right. Even though he won't admit it, I'm pretty sure he's the one who sent those hombres after you tonight."

She nodded, not looking surprised by what he said. "Were they the ones who shot at you right after I came in the hotel? I heard the shots, of course, and then later I saw you in the street talking to the marshal, so I thought you must have been involved."

"Yeah, they tried to bushwhack me, all right," Fargo said. "The same four gents. The one called Elam, the one who grabbed your arm, got away. The other three didn't."

Her eyes widened. "You killed them?"

"Seemed like the thing to do at the time."

She looked down at the floor and shook her head. "I knew Father and Mr. Stoddard were rivals, competitors. I knew Mr. Stoddard was angry because Father bested him on several business deals. But when we came to Los Angeles I didn't know it was going to be so dangerous."

Fargo inclined his head toward the room next door. "You reckon your father is still up?"

25

"I'm sure he is. I said good night to him just a little while ago, and he was poring over his maps."

"Obliged," Fargo said. "I'd like to talk to him."

Hope sprang up in her eyes. "You'd like to work for us? For him, I mean."

"Stoddard rubbed me the wrong way," Fargo admitted.

She reached out and put a hand on his arm. "Come in. I'll tell Father you're here."

Fargo had planned to just knock on the door of room twenty and introduce himself to Arthur Grayson, but he supposed Belinda's suggestion would work, too. He stepped into the room and she closed the door behind him.

She went straight to the door of the adjoining room and tapped on it, then opened it without waiting for an answer. "Father," she said, "Mr. Skye Fargo is here."

"Fargo!" The exclamation came from the other room. Fargo heard a chair scrape, and then a stocky man with gray hair and a mustache appeared in the doorway. Compact and muscular, he wore the trousers from a dark suit with a white shirt that had the sleeves rolled up and the collar open. Fargo liked him on sight.

Arthur Grayson came toward Fargo with his hand outstretched. "The Trailsman, as I live and breathe," he said. "It's an honor to meet you, sir."

"Pleased to meet you, too, Mr. Grayson," Fargo said as he shook hands with the man.

"You were recommended to me by several of my associates," Grayson went on. "I'd hoped to get in touch with you and offer you a job, but then Belinda told me she had run into you and said you were here to talk to Hiram Stoddard, so I thought I didn't have a chance of hiring you."

"I'm not going to work for Stoddard," Fargo said. "Doesn't mean I'm looking for another job, though."

"But you're here. Surely that means you'll entertain the idea."

"I wouldn't mind knowing what your plans are," Fargo admitted.

Grayson took hold of his arm. The man had a firm grip. "Come into my room. I'll show you the maps. And I've got some decent brandy, too, if you'd like a drink."

Fargo had turned down the brandy Stoddard offered him. But he had turned down Stoddard's job, too, he reminded himself.

"Don't mind if I do," he told Grayson with a nod.

The man turned to his daughter and said, "Thank you for introducing me to Mr. Fargo, my dear. We'll try to keep our voices down so our discussion won't disturb your sleep."

"What are you talking about, Father? I'm going to be here, too."

Grayson frowned. "Surely a lot of business talk would just be boring for you."

"Not at all. You know I take a great interest in your business."

For a second Grayson looked like he wanted to argue, but he must have known it would be hopeless to do so. He shrugged and said, "If you're going to join us, at least put on something more, ah, appropriate."

Belinda smiled in triumph. "I'll be there in a moment."

Grayson led Fargo into the other room and shut the door. He waved a hand toward a table covered with unrolled maps. Various small items weighted down their corners and held them open.

"Take a look at those while I pour the drinks," Grayson invited.

Fargo hung his hat on the back of a chair and went to the table. He bent over to study the maps, which he recognized as U.S. topographical surveys of various parts of California. A large map of the entire state lay on the table, too. Someone had marked points that lay in a line up the coast from San Diego to Sonoma, north of San Francisco.

Grayson brought snifters of brandy from a side-board similar to the one in Stoddard's room. As he handed one of the glasses to Fargo, he said, "That's the Old Mission Trail marked on the state map."

Fargo nodded. "I'm familiar with it. I've been to most of the missions, in fact."

Earlier in California's history, over a period of a little more than fifty years while it was still under Spanish rule, Franciscan friars had established the string of twenty-one missions, each of them about a day's walk from the next. Towns, or pueblos, as the Spaniards called them, had grown up around many of those missions. The trail linking them had been a vital part of civilization's development in the state.

But the route laid out by the friars had been designed with walking in mind. A stage line couldn't follow every twist and turn of the trail. Also, in some places the terrain was too rugged for wheeled vehicles, even though a man on foot or horseback would be able to negotiate it.

That was why whoever established the first major stage line along the coast would need to lay out a new route that followed the Old Mission Trail in some stretches but not in others. That was why Arthur Grayson needed the services of someone like the Trailsman.

As Fargo sipped the brandy, Grayson traced the

route on the map with a blunt fingertip. "I have coaches parked in a wagon yard here in town, ready to go," he said. "Whoever takes one up the coast first will have a leg up on the competition. That's why I'd like for you to lead it through, Mr. Fargo, and I'll pay well if you agree to do so."

Fargo frowned and said, "Wait a minute. I thought you were just looking for someone to lay out the route. I didn't know you were planning to make a run right now."

Grayson nodded. "Absolutely. What better way to prove it can be done in a timely and efficient manner?"

"You realize there's some pretty wild country between here and there? Until the route is laid out, and a road cleared and graded in places, a coach might run into some danger."

"I know there's a risk. There usually is when you're talking about doing something worthwhile."

Fargo couldn't argue with that. The job Grayson described was a little bigger than Fargo had reckoned on, though. It wasn't just a scouting chore. Whoever led that coach up the coast would be responsible for getting it where it was going, safe and sound.

The door to the adjoining room opened. Belinda came in wearing a conservative dark blue dress that made her look more her age, rather than younger, as the colorful Mexican garb had done. She was no less attractive for that, though.

"Have you and Mr. Fargo come to an arrangement yet, Father?" she asked.

"I think he's still pondering on it," Grayson said.

Fargo nodded. "That's right."

Belinda came over to Fargo and said, "Father has told you that one of our coaches will be going up the coast right away, as the route is being determined?"

"He has."

"Will it help you make up your mind to know that I intend to be one of the passengers on that coach?"

"Blast it, Belinda," her father said. "You know I haven't agreed to that."

"I know you're planning to go, and I'm not going to let you go alone."

"I'd feel a lot better about everything if I knew you were safe here in Los Angeles."

So would Fargo. Grayson's plans were already turning out to be more of a challenge than he had anticipated. The addition of both Belinda and Grayson as passengers on the first coach would just make things more difficult.

But at the same time, what he had just learned made it more difficult for Fargo to refuse Grayson's offer. Grayson was determined to go through with his plans whether Fargo agreed to help or not; Fargo could tell that from the man's attitude.

Without an experienced scout and guide such as himself, the stagecoach trip up the coast would be even more dangerous for everyone involved. Could he turn his back on that situation and let things proceed without doing everything he could to help?

Fargo knew the answer to that question.

"Neither of you should go along," he said, doubting that his advice would change their minds. "And you shouldn't send a coach up there until the whole route has been laid out and prepared."

Grayson shook his head. "I can't wait. If I do, Stoddard will beat me to it. He'll get the mail contracts, the delivery contracts, the passengers. He'll have the whole thing clutched right in his greedy fist."

Fargo could have made the argument that Grayson wanted to get the jump on Stoddard, just as Stoddard wanted to beat him to the punch. Neither man had any sort of moral right to be first in this game.

But Stoddard was the one who had resorted to kidnapping a young woman to get what he wanted, or at least trying to. Fargo's instincts told him that while Grayson would fight hard to win, he would also fight fair.

"What do you say, Mr. Fargo?" Grayson asked. "I hate to put pressure on you like this, but I need your help if I'm going to have any chance to succeed. Stoddard will do anything to stop me."

Fargo didn't doubt that. Somewhat against his better judgment, he nodded.

"All right," he said. "I'll throw in with you. But once we start out, I'm in charge. Is that understood?"

Belinda and Grayson were both smiling at Fargo's decision. Grayson said, "Understood, Mr. Fargo."

"Might as well call me Skye, if we're going to be working together."

Belinda said, "Now I'm really looking forward to this trip . . . Skye."

Fargo spent the next couple of hours in Grayson's hotel room, the two of them going over the maps by lamplight. Belinda sat with them for a while, but then she grew tired and returned to her room to go to bed.

Fargo asked Grayson as many questions as he could think of about the operation, and he had to admit that Grayson seemed to know what he was doing. The man had set up several successful stage lines in Missouri, Kansas, and Texas, and they had made him comfortably wealthy.

Grayson was risking much of his wealth on this California venture, though, so he had a lot riding on it.

Fargo left the hotel after midnight, tired from the

long ride to Los Angeles and the eventful evening after he got there. He was ready to slip into the bunk that Pablo would have waiting for him in the back room of the cantina.

The door was closed and the front part of the building was dark when Fargo got there. He walked around behind it and slipped inside through the rear door. A single candle in a wall holder gave off just enough light for Fargo to make his way along the corridor to the door of the room he always used when he stayed at Pablo's.

The room itself was dark, but when Fargo opened the door, enough light from the candle spilled inside for him to be able to see the bunk under the window.

He saw the shape lying there under a thin sheet and recognized the curves as female. The sound of deep, regular breathing came from her.

With a sigh, Fargo eased the door shut behind him. He dug a match out of his pocket, snapped the lucifer to life with his thumbnail, and held the flame to the wick of a candle on a tiny bedside table. When the candle was burning, he said, "Sofia!"

His voice was sharp enough to rouse the girl from sleep. She sat up and gasped, the sheet sliding away from her naked body. In the candlelight, her dusky skin, wild tangle of black hair, and dark eyes, wide with surprise, gave her the look of a pagan. A pagan lover—that was what she wanted to be, and Skye Fargo was her quarry.

Her body had been lush even at fourteen, almost a woman's body. Now, five years later, maturity made her a very beautiful woman indeed. Her breasts were high and full and firm, crowned with dark brown nipples. Her face held an earthy, sultry quality that proclaimed, just as surely as her body, that she was made to please a man in bed.

But when Fargo looked at her, a part of him saw not a sensuous young woman but rather the little girl she had been when he first met her.

"Senor Skye," she said, "You frightened me!"

"You scared me a mite, too, Sofia," Fargo told her. Her full lips curved in a smile. "How could I ever frighten a man such as you, Senor Skye?"

"By climbing into my bed uninvited. If you keep this up, Sofia, one of these days I'm going to take what you keep offering me."

That was the wrong thing to say, he realized, as she smiled even more and pushed the sheet back to swing her legs out of the bunk and stand up. She was nude, and a gorgeous sight to behold, from her muscular calves up the sleek columns of her thighs, to the thick triangle of dark hair at the base of her slightly rounded belly, those magnificent breasts, and the face that was set in an expression of sleepy lust.

"It is yours any time you want it," she said. "You know that, *mi corazón.*"

"Right now what I need is some sleep, so put your clothes on and get out of here." He didn't want to hurt her feelings, but he wanted it made clear that she wasn't going to accomplish her goal tonight.

Instead of reaching for the skirt and blouse she had tossed over the room's single chair, she came toward him and stopped just in front of him, close enough so that the hard tips of her breasts brushed the front of his buckskin shirt.

"Senor Skye," she said as she laid her hands on his shoulders, "you might as well surrender. Tonight you will be mine. The time has come for us to be together."

She came up on her toes and pressed her mouth to his.

With steely resolve, Fargo tried not to respond to

her. That lasted about five seconds. Then his arms came up and went around her, pulling her against him. Her body molded to his. Her lips were hot and fierce and demanding.

Fargo had deflowered a few virgins in his time, back when he was a young man, but no matter how ardently Sofia was offering herself to him, he felt uneasy about it. She might hope that he would stay with her, when they both knew that was impossible. He might settle down someday, if he lived long enough, but that time was still far in the future.

He pulled his head back, breaking the kiss, and growled, "Damn it, get out of here. This isn't right."

"If it is not right, then why are you still holding me?"

He let go of her. She clutched at him, but he stepped back. As he did, his foot bumped something on the floor, something he hadn't noticed when he came in because he'd been distracted by discovering Sofia in his bed. He looked down and saw a box about a foot square and six inches deep on the floor.

"Where'd that come from?" he asked.

"What?" Sofia was still upset by his rejection of her, so she didn't seem to understand what he was talking about at first. Then she looked down at the box and said, "Oh, that. It was on the bed when I came in. I thought Pablo put it there. Some tortillas, probably, in case you are hungry." Her bottom lip came out in a pout. "I would rather you were hungry for me."

"You moved it off the bed?"

"*Sí.*"

Fargo prodded the box again. A humming sound came from it. He leaned closer and listened, realizing that what he heard wasn't humming at all.

It was a fast, low-pitched rattle.

4

Fargo's left hand shot out to stop Sofia as she started to take a step toward him again. His right dropped to the butt of the Colt on his hip, but he didn't draw the gun just yet.

"Senor Skye! What is it? What is wrong?"

"Stay back," Fargo told her. "If what's in this box is what I think it is, you don't want any part of it." He licked his lips, which had gone dry. "Neither do I, but I don't have much choice in the matter."

"Skye, I am frightened—"

"You should be." Fargo felt cold inside when he thought about Sofia picking up the box and moving it off the bunk without an idea in her head except how she planned to seduce him.

She wouldn't have been very seductive if he had come in and found her dead.

He studied the box. It was flimsy, made of thin strips of wood interlaced together. The lid was hinged but not fastened in any way. Fargo steeled his nerves and reached down to take hold of it. His thumbs looped over the lid to make sure that it stayed closed.

The rattle grew louder as Fargo picked up the box and carried it toward the window, moving with great caution as he did so. "Stay back," he told Sofia again.

"If I drop this, or if it busts open, jump onto the bed as fast as you can and start yelling for help."

"That sound . . . it is what I think it is?"

Fargo nodded. "Yep."

He reached the window, leaned out into the night, and tilted the box so that when he let go of the lid, it would fall open away from him. Breathing a little easier once he was in that position, he said to Sofia, "Bring the candle over here and hold it so the light shines outside."

She did so, leaning into the window beside him. Her face was tight with nervousness, and neither of them paid any attention anymore to the fact that she was still naked.

"Hold the candle steady," Fargo breathed. He lifted his thumbs to release the lid of the box.

It fell open, and the snake that had been inside the box tumbled out to land in the dirt just outside the window. The rattle on the end of its tail was still buzzing in furious anger.

Fargo tossed the empty box aside as the snake fell. He drew his Colt with blinding speed, so that the revolver was in his hand by the time the snake hit the ground. Instead of coiling, as Fargo had hoped it would, it began twisting away in a distinctive motion. He took aim in the candlelight and pulled the trigger twice.

The second shot exploded the snake's head, spraying its gory remains across the alley behind the cantina. Fargo felt a certain atavistic satisfaction as he saw the now headless body whipping around in its death throes, the same surge of savage triumph man always experienced at the death of a snake. The feeling went back as far as the Garden of Eden, Fargo reckoned.

"Dios mio," Sofia said. "It was a sidewinder."

"Yeah," Fargo said. Smaller than a diamondback but no less deadly. He knew it had been coiled in the box when someone placed it on the bed.

Not Pablo, though, as Sofia had assumed. Whoever had tried to kill him had reached in through the open window and placed the box on the bed. If Fargo had come in and laid down without lighting the candle, he would have crushed the box and set the snake free to strike him. If he had seen it first, the would-be killer had hoped he would open it to take a look inside.

"Who could have done such a thing?" Sofia asked. She put a hand to her mouth in terrified realization. "*Dios mio*, I picked it up and moved it—"

A hammering on the door interrupted her. "Skye!" Pablo's heavy voice called. "Skye, are you all right?" The shots must have awakened the cantina's proprietor.

"Cover up if you're going to," Fargo said to Sofia as he went to the door. She wasted no time pulling the sheet off the bed and wrapping herself in it.

Pablo didn't look surprised to see Sofia when Fargo opened the door. "I heard shots," he grumbled as he stepped into the room carrying a lantern. With a glare at Sofia, he added, "Were you trying to drive away something troublesome?"

"You could say that," Fargo replied. "Take a look out the window."

Appearing puzzled, Pablo carried the lantern to the window, leaned out, and exclaimed as he saw the rattlesnake's body in the alley.

"See that box lying out there?" Fargo went on. "Somebody put the snake in it, reached through the window, and left it on the bed for me, like a present. It wasn't one that I wanted, though."

Pablo turned around to face him. "But who . . . who would do such a thing?"

Fargo had been in Los Angeles only a few hours on this visit, and the only enemies he had made so far were Hiram Stoddard and the hardcase called Elam. He thought that either of them were capable of trying to kill him. He had interfered with their plans, and vengeance was the spur that drove men like them.

Chances were Stoddard hadn't handled the chore himself. He wasn't the sort to go around catching rattlesnakes and putting them in boxes. He might have come up with the idea, but he would have ordered Elam or another of his flunkies to carry it out.

"I've got a pretty good idea who's to blame," Fargo said. "What I'm wondering is how anybody knew I was going to be staying in this room."

Pablo gave an expressive shrug of his shoulders. "The cantina is a busy place," he said. "Many men were at the bar when we were talking earlier. Anyone could have heard me say that your usual room would be made ready for you, and perhaps someone questioned one of my serving girls to find out which room that is."

Fargo thought about it and nodded. The theory Pablo suggested made sense. In fact, it was the only explanation that did . . . unless someone who worked at the cantina was responsible for the attempt on his life, and none of them had any reason to want him dead.

If Pablo was right, that meant someone who worked for Stoddard had been here tonight. Again, there was nothing unusual in that. The cantina was one of the pueblo's popular watering holes. Plenty of gringos as well as Mexicans drank there.

"Would you like a different room for the night?" Pablo asked.

Fargo thought about it and shook his head. "I don't reckon anything else will happen tonight."

"Very well. I will take the snake's body and toss it into the river." Pablo cast another glance at Sofia and went out.

She said, "Senor Skye, after what happened, I do not think that I . . . that I feel like . . . You understand?"

"Sure," he told her. "I'm not much in the mood myself anymore." He leaned over and gave her a quick kiss on the forehead. "Grab your clothes and skedaddle. Maybe there'll be another time for us."

He doubted it, though. Sooner or later Sofia would figure out that she needed to find somebody else better suited to her.

As for Fargo, even though the danger had made him more alert for a while, he was getting sleepy again. He undressed and lay down with his gun close at hand.

But not before pulling the bed away from the window so that nobody could reach inside and drop another sidewinder on him.

Fargo was up early the next morning, breakfasting on tortillas, eggs, and chili peppers in Pablo's kitchen, washed down with strong black coffee flavored with chocolate. The rest of the night had passed quietly, and Fargo felt rested.

He checked on the Ovaro, then walked to the hotel to see Grayson and Belinda. If they were going to go ahead with their plans, he saw no point in delaying.

Fargo ran into Grayson in the hotel lobby. The man had just emerged from the dining room, where he'd had his own breakfast. He greeted Fargo with a grin and a handshake.

"I was just coming to look you up," Grayson said. "Thought you might like to see the coach and meet the driver."

"That's what I had in mind, too," Fargo agreed with a nod.

Together, the two men left the hotel and walked down the street. Grayson led the way to a wagon yard where three stagecoaches were parked.

"They're not straight from the Abbott and Downing Company factory at Concord, New Hampshire," Grayson said as he waved a hand at the vehicles. "I bought them from the Butterfield Line, rather than trying to bring coaches out here from one of my other lines back east. But they're in good shape, and I've had men going over them, making any necessary repairs."

Fargo went into the wagon yard and walked around the coaches, making a close inspection of them, especially the broad leather thoroughbraces that ran under the body of each coach. Those thoroughbraces supported the coaches and acted as shock absorbers of a sort, although anyone who had ridden very far on a stage knew they didn't absorb anywhere near all of the bumps and jolts.

The thoroughbraces were in good shape, as Grayson had said, and so were the singletrees to which the horses in the teams would be attached when they were hitched up. Fresh coats of red and yellow paint had been slapped on the vehicles. The brass fittings had been polished.

The stagecoaches wouldn't look that nice after they had finished the long, hard run up the coast. By the time they got where they were going, they would be covered with a thick layer of dust, and the paint would be scratched and scraped in quite a few places.

Fargo gave a nod of approval to Grayson and said, "Looks like the coaches are ready to roll. Where's the jehu you've hired?"

"He should be around," Grayson said with a frown. "I'll ask the fellow who owns the wagon yard."

He went in the office and came back out in a moment with a grim look on his face. "The man said to check in the barn."

Grayson stalked in that direction. Fargo followed, trying to suppress a smile. From the sound of Grayson's voice, he hadn't liked what the proprietor of the wagon yard had told him.

The barn's big double doors were open. Grayson went inside, looked around, and called, "Mr. Stevens! Mr. Stevens, are you in here?"

Fargo heard some sort of incoherent mutter from the hayloft and pointed a thumb in that direction. "Sounds like he's up there."

Grayson tilted his head back and said, "Mr. Stevens, if you're up there, please come down!"

After some rustling around in the hay, a wild tangle of graying hair thrust itself over the edge of the loft. "Who's that?" the man under the hair called. His bleary gaze roamed around the shadowy interior of the barn for a second or two before it focused on Grayson and Fargo. "Oh, Mr. Grayson!" the man went on. "Howdy! Just hang on, and I'll be right there."

More rustling. Stevens must have been looking for his hat, because a battered old hat with the brim pushed up in front was crammed on his head as he reappeared and began climbing down the ladder from the loft.

He had some trouble with that, slipping several times and almost falling. Each time he had to clutch the ladder for a moment before he could start down again. Fargo tried not to chuckle. He recognized a hell of a hangover when he saw one.

The man finally reached the bottom of the ladder. He still clung to one of the rungs to steady himself as he turned toward Fargo and Grayson. In addition to

41

the hat, he wore a red flannel shirt with leather sleeve cuffs, a buckskin vest, patched denim trousers, and down-at-the-heel boots. Fargo put his age around forty. His short beard was streaked with gray, and his skin was leathery from years of exposure to sun and wind.

"This is Mr. Stevens," Grayson said to Fargo with a note of disapproval in his voice. "I've engaged him to drive the stagecoach up the coast on this inaugural run."

"Call me Sandy," Stevens said. He looked like he wanted to shake hands, but he realized that his right hand was still holding on to the ladder. He switched hands and thrust out a callused palm.

Fargo shook hands with the man and said, "The moon was shining bright on pretty red wings last night, eh, Sandy?"

"You're damn right about that, mister. Bright as it could be. I didn't catch your handle."

"Skye Fargo."

Bleary or not, Sandy's eyes opened wider. "The Trailsman?"

"One and the same."

Grayson put in, "Mr. Fargo's going to lay out the route for us and guide the coach on the first run."

"I told you it'd be a good idea to find the Trailsman and hire him. I've heard a bunch o' stories 'bout you, Fargo."

"Most of them aren't true," Fargo said.

Sandy chuckled. "Hell, if even half of 'em are, you been to see the elephant, son."

"How soon can we get started?" Grayson asked.

Sandy blinked at him. "Headin' for San Francisco, you mean?"

"That's right. Mr. Fargo and I agree that it's not a good idea to wait any longer than necessary. That just gives Hiram Stoddard more time to try to stop us."

Sandy was a little steadier on his feet now. He let go of the ladder and used that hand to scratch at his beard. He pulled something out of the thicket of hair, looked at it, and flicked it aside.

"You're the boss," he said with a shrug. "We'll go when you say to go."

"Yes, but aren't there preparations to be made?"

"Them coaches are fit as fiddles," Sandy said. "I got two teams o' horses picked out. Since they ain't no stage stations betwixt here an' there, we'll take our fresh team with us. Found a boy to wrangle 'em for us, I did. O' course, we might be able to pick up some spare animals at one o' them pueblos along the way, but just in case we can't we'll have two teams we can switch out."

Fargo nodded. He had wondered about that very thing. The common practice was to change teams every eight to ten miles. They wouldn't have that luxury on this run, but neither could they expect the same horses to pull the coach all the way from Los Angeles to San Francisco. And from time to time they would have to stop to rest both teams of horses.

Finding suitable locations for stage stations was another part of laying out the route for the line. Fargo had handled that chore on several occasions in the past. He couldn't help but think that Arthur Grayson was rushing things here, but he understood the man's reasons for doing so.

Fargo just hoped that getting in a hurry wouldn't come back to cause trouble for them before they reached their destination.

"All right," Grayson said. "Considering everything I've heard, I think we should leave this afternoon."

"That quick, huh?" Sandy said. He shrugged again. "You're the boss."

"You'll be, ah, sufficiently recovered by then?"

"You mean from this hangover I got?" Sandy

snorted in derision. "Hell, it ain't nothin'. I've had lots worse. All I need is a little hair o' the dog, a shot or two of that who-hit-John—"

"There'll be no more drinking," Grayson declared. "Not until we get to San Francisco."

"No more—" Sandy choked as he stared at his employer. He jerked the old hat off his head and began wadding it up in agitation. "You didn't say nothin' 'bout how I couldn't take no jug along."

"That's one of my rules," Grayson insisted. "None of my drivers on my other lines drinks while handling the reins. I can try to find someone else if you'd like, but I was told that you're a good driver . . . when you're sober."

"Yeah, but I'm better drunk," Sandy muttered. He sighed in acceptance of Grayson's terms. "All right, if that's the way it's got to be, then I reckon I'll have to live with it. I need the dinero. I . . . uh . . . run up a pretty big tab at one o' the whorehouses. Mama Graciela, she made me promise I'd pay her when I get back. Otherwise she was gonna take a bowie knife an' go to carvin' off items that are mighty precious to me. To hold 'em for security, she said. Hell, without them, what need would I have to ever even go back to a whorehouse, I ask you!"

Grayson didn't attempt to answer that question, and Fargo figured it would be wise if he didn't, either.

After attending the inquest for the three hombres he had killed the night before—all of whom were ruled by the coroner's jury to have met their deaths in a justifiable manner—Fargo ate dinner with Grayson and Belinda at the hotel. Then he helped them carry their bags down to the wagon yard to load them in the boot on the back of one of the Concord coaches. Fargo had held out a little hope that Belinda might have changed her mind about going along, but he wasn't surprised that she hadn't. She was a determined young woman.

Fargo had already said adios to Pablo and a disappointed Sofia. "I will be waiting for you when you get back, Senor Skye," she had promised him.

Fargo didn't doubt that for a second, much as he might have wished it was otherwise.

When they arrived at the wagon yard, Sandy was supervising the hostlers, who were hitching up a good-looking six-horse team. Six more sturdy horses were roped together as a group that could be led by one man. When Fargo finished stowing the luggage in the boot, Sandy introduced him to the wrangler.

"This here's Jimmy," Sandy said, nodding toward a lanky young man with thick blond hair sticking out from under a brown hat with a round crown.

"Call me Joaquin," the youngster said as he shook hands with Fargo.

"I thought Sandy said your name was Jimmy."

"It is, but call me Joaquin. Like Joaquin Murrieta. You heard of Joaquin Murrieta? The famous stagecoach robber and highwayman? I'm gonna be just like him one of these days."

Fargo looked at Sandy. "You hired somebody who wants to be a bandit to work for a stagecoach line?"

"Oh, don't pay no attention to him. He's good with horses, but other'n that he ain't right in the head. Anyway, if he wants to be a bandit, I figure I'd rather have him with us than agin us."

"Stand and deliver," Jimmy said. "Stand and deliver."

Fargo stood there, all right, but instead of delivering, he thought about what he had gotten himself into. Not only did he have to lay out the best route through some wild, rugged, and even dangerous country, but he also had to ride herd on a businessman, a stubborn young woman, a jehu with a fondness for rotgut, and a youngster who might well be a little touched in the head.

Jimmy—or Joaquin—might not be the only one that description applied to. Fargo had to wonder if he was a mite crazy himself to take on this chore.

But he had said that he would do it, and he wasn't the sort of man to go back on his word.

"Let's go to San Francisco," he said.

5

From San Gabriel Arcángel, the mission near Los Angeles, the original trail ran northwest to San Fernando Rey de España and San Buenaventura. This route led through the Santa Monica Mountains that overlooked the pueblo in that direction, but although the path was steep in places, it was wide and well defined, so the stagecoach had no trouble following it. The horses were strong and fresh and hauled the coach up the slopes without much difficulty.

Riding the Ovaro, Fargo ranged ahead, staying about a hundred yards in front of the coach most of the time. He kept his eyes open, knowing that Hiram Stoddard was capable of hiring men to ambush them.

No one tried to waylay them, though, and the journey got off to a good start. They stopped for the night at San Buenaventura. Fargo was pleased with the progress they had made, considering that they hadn't gotten started until the afternoon.

He knew they were a long way from being out of the woods, though. He didn't think Stoddard would let them make it all the way to San Francisco without trying to stop them—by killing them if necessary.

A pueblo had not been established at Buenaventura, but a small village called Ventura was near the mission from which it had taken its name. Sandy brought the coach to a halt in front of a cantina that had a stable next door. He leaned over and called through the window of the vehicle, "Everybody out! Jimmy an' me will tend to the horses whilst you folks go on inside."

Fargo had ridden back to join the others. He swung down from the saddle as Grayson and Belinda were climbing out of the coach.

Belinda cast a rather skeptical glance at the squat adobe building and asked, "Is this where we're going to spend the night?"

"This settlement isn't very big," Fargo told her. "Chances are the best accommodations it has to offer are right here."

"All right," she said. "If you say so, Skye."

Later on, once the stagecoach line was established and the route was set, the coaches would travel at night as well as during the day, at least over parts of the line. Some stretches of the route might be too treacherous for nighttime travel. But since the final path hadn't been determined yet, daylight was required for Fargo to decide exactly where the coach would go next.

Fargo led the Ovaro into the stable and refused the elderly Mexican hostler's offer of assistance as he unsaddled and rubbed down the stallion, then made sure the horse had plenty of grain and water. He returned to the cantina to find Grayson and Belinda sitting at a table in the corner and casting nervous glances around them.

"Mr. Stevens claimed we would be safe in here," Grayson said, "but I'm not so sure. Some of those men at the bar look like cutthroats."

To Fargo the men Grayson referred to looked more like vaqueros from the nearby ranches. He said, "I don't think you have anything to worry about. They just want to drink their tequila in peace after a hard day's work."

"Well, if you say so." Grayson didn't sound convinced, though.

Sandy and Jimmy came in a short time later, having tended to the horses and gotten them fed, watered, and stabled. As the two men joined Fargo, Grayson, and Belinda at the table, Sandy smacked his lips and declared, "I could do with a jug o' tequila. Is that allowed now that we're stopped for the night, Mr. Grayson?"

"I'd rather you didn't get a jug," Grayson replied. "You might be sick in the morning if you drank that much, like you were today. But I suppose it would be all right for you to have a drink or two with supper."

"Shoot, that's better'n nothin'," Sandy said, grinning in anticipation.

A serving girl brought them a platter full of tortillas, along with bowls of beans, strips of spicy beef, and several kinds of peppers. Everyone was hungry and dug in. Belinda was soon gasping and waving a hand in front of her mouth.

"My goodness, this food is hot," she said. She reached for the nearest of what appeared to be cups of water that the girl had placed on the table as well.

"Careful," Fargo warned, but even as he spoke Belinda took a big gulp from the cup. She gasped and choked but managed to swallow. Her face paled and her eyes grew huge.

"What . . . what in heaven's name was that?" she asked when she could talk again.

"Tequila," Fargo told her. "Take it a little slower. The stuff still packs a kick, but it won't burn your insides out if you don't gulp it."

"Now if you're like me," Sandy said, "you're lucky

and got a cast-iron gullet. That stuff goes down smooth as branch water for me."

He proved it by taking a long swallow from his cup, licking his lips, and sighing in satisfaction.

"Eat a tortilla," Fargo told Belinda as he pushed the platter toward her. "That'll cut the pepper's burn a mite."

As the meal proceeded, Fargo, Grayson, and Sandy discussed the part of the trail they had covered so far and the ground they would go over the next day. Fargo had ridden the Old Mission Trail before and had an uncanny ability to remember any path he had ever gone over, so he had a good idea what they would be facing. The route was pretty easy here along the coast and wouldn't grow more rugged for another day or two.

Several men came into the cantina while the group was eating. Fargo eyed them as they went to the bar and ordered drinks. They were white, and while they might have been cowboys from one of the neighboring ranches, they didn't really have the look of men who worked with cattle.

They looked more like the same sort of hardcases as had been working for Hiram Stoddard in Los Angeles.

The newcomers seemed to pay no attention to the group of pilgrims at the table in the corner. Fargo didn't trust them, though, and he leaned over to say to Sandy, "One of us better plan on spending the night in the stable so we can keep an eye on the coach and those horses."

Despite the two cups of tequila the jehu had downed, he was clear-eyed and alert. He nodded and said, "I reckon you're right about that, Fargo. I was just thinkin' the same thing."

"Is there a problem?" Grayson asked.

"Not so far," Fargo told him. "We want it to stay that way."

They went on with their meal, and the men at the bar continued drinking. Jimmy asked, "Did you ever hear about the big shoot-out between Joaquin Murrieta and Captain Harry Love, Mr. Fargo? They say Joaquin was killed during the battle between his men and Captain Love's rangers, but I don't believe it. That head in the jar they said was Joaquin's couldn't have been his."

"I've met Harry Love, Jimmy," Fargo said. "He claims it really was Joaquin's head, and Captain Love is an honorable man. I'd be inclined to give him the benefit of the doubt."

Jimmy shook his head. "Nope. Joaquin was too slick a bandit to get caught like that. I'll bet he's down in Mexico right now, livin' the good life."

Fargo smiled. It wouldn't do any harm to indulge the youngster. "Maybe you're right, Jimmy," he said.

"I'm gonna get some more beans," Jimmy said as he pushed back his chair and stood up.

"Go easy on them things," Sandy called after him as Jimmy started toward the bar. "You'll be playin' the bugle all night." He glanced at Belinda, who was blushing. "Beggin' your pardon, ma'am."

As Jimmy approached the bar, one of the men standing there turned away, and his action put him right in Jimmy's path. Their shoulders collided.

"Damn it!" the man burst out. "Watch where you're goin', you stupid bastard."

"Uh-oh," Sandy said under his breath.

Fargo had already taken note of what was going on and wasn't surprised by it. He had thought ever since the men entered the cantina that they might be here to cause trouble. They had been waiting for the right opportunity—and Jimmy had just given it to them.

"I'm sorry, mister," the youngster said. "I didn't mean to run into you. But come to think of it, it was really you who run into me."

The man glared at him. "What the hell did you just say?"

"I said it was you who run into me. But that's all right. Wasn't no harm done."

"I'll be the one to say whether or not any harm was done," the man replied, sticking out his jaw in a belligerent fashion. "And I don't like it when some half-wit kid argues with me."

Jimmy frowned. "I ain't no half-wit. I just ain't had much schoolin', and I never learned to think so good."

"You're a damn stupid jackass—that's what you are."

Over at the table, Grayson watched the confrontation with a worried frown on his face and said, "Skye, shouldn't we do something about this?"

"I intend to," Fargo said as he rose to his feet. He glanced down at the jehu. "Sandy?"

"Don't worry," Sandy said as he touched the butt of the heavy cap-and-ball pistol he carried in a crossdraw holster on his left hip. "I'll keep an eye on them other varmints."

Fargo nodded and walked toward the bar. The hardcase was still cursing Jimmy, and as Fargo approached, the man gave the youngster a hard shove.

Jimmy caught his balance before he fell. His face was twisted up like he didn't know whether to get mad or cry. "Hey!" he said. "I told you I was sorry, mister. You got no call to get rough with me."

"You said it was my fault," the man rasped. "I'm gonna teach you—"

"You're not going to teach him anything," Fargo said as he stepped between Jimmy and the hardcase.

"But he could teach you something, hombre . . . like how to be a decent human being."

"Who the hell are you?"

If the man was working for Hiram Stoddard, chances were he already knew who Fargo was. But Fargo answered anyway, saying, "I'm a friend of his, and I don't like the way you're treating him."

The hardcase's mouth twisted in a sneer. "Why don't you do something about it, then?" he demanded.

The other men had moved away from the bar and were edging closer. Fargo said, "You might tell your partners to have a look at the older fella over there at the table where I was sitting."

The hardcase's eyes flicked past Fargo's shoulder in that direction. Fargo heard the metallic ratcheting as Sandy eared back the hammer on his big hogleg. He'd had a hunch that Sandy had drawn the gun by now, and he was glad to hear that he was right.

"Damn it—" the hardcase started to say.

"This is between you and me, hombre," Fargo cut in. "If any of the others try to take a hand, they're liable to get a hole the size of a fist blown through them."

The man pointed at Jimmy. "He's the one started it! You got no call to mix in. It ain't your fight!"

"He's my friend, so I'm making it my fight."

"Mr. Fargo." Jimmy pawed at Fargo's shoulder. "Mr. Fargo, you don't have to go gettin' in a ruckus on my account. I'm sorry I caused trouble."

Fargo turned his head to smile at the youngster. "You didn't cause any trouble, Jimmy," he assured him. "This doesn't have—"

Jimmy's eyes widened. "Look out, Mr. Fargo!"

Not surprised that the hardcase was trying to strike the first blow while he wasn't looking, Fargo twisted around to face the man again. He saw the fist coming at him and weaved to one side. The punch sailed wide and the hardcase stumbled, thrown off balance by the missed blow.

Fargo stepped in and hooked a hard, fast left into the man's belly. The hardcase's breath, sour with tequila fumes, gusted out of his mouth as he bent over and took a step backward. He recovered in a hurry and swung a wild, looping left at Fargo's head.

The punch would have done some damage if it had connected, but once again Fargo avoided it, stepping back so that the knobby fist passed in front of his face. He snapped a stinging right jab to the hardcase's nose. The man grunted in pain as blood spurted.

"Get him, Robey!" one of the hardcase's companions urged. "Tear the bastard in two!"

Robey was a big man with heavy shoulders and long arms, a grizzly to Fargo's panther. He used the back of his hand to swipe some of the blood off his face and roared in anger. When he lunged at Fargo again, he didn't throw another punch. Instead his arms were outstretched to trap the Trailsman and pull him into a bone-crushing bear hug.

Once again, though, Fargo's speed allowed him to elude the attack. He ducked under Robey's grasping arms and reached up to grab hold of one of them. Twisting his body, he hauled hard on the arm as he threw a hip into Robey's midsection. Despite his size, Robey's feet came off the floor. He shouted in surprise as he sailed through the air to come crashing down on his back.

For a moment Robey lay there unmoving, and Fargo thought he was going to stay down. But then the hardcase rolled over, got his hands and knees under him, and shook his head to clear the cobwebs from his brain. The motion made crimson droplets from his smashed nose splatter on the puncheon floor under him.

He pushed himself to his feet and glared at Fargo. His face was dark with rage. As he reached behind his back, he said in a thick voice, "That's it. I'm gonna carve you, you son of a bitch."

He brought out a long, heavy-bladed bowie knife from a sheath at the small of his back.

Fargo reached down and drew the Arkansas tooth-pick from the fringed sheath strapped to his calf. The blade was even longer than that of the bowie, and just as heavy.

"You don't have to do this," he said.

"The hell I don't," Robey grated. "Gonna cut you in little pieces."

His friends called encouragement to him as he launched his attack on Fargo, but they stayed where they were, kept back by the threat of that cap-and-ball in Sandy's hand. The light from the cantina's lamps winked on the two blades as they came together with the ring of cold steel. Sparks flew.

Fargo was an experienced knife fighter, but so was his opponent. Robey thrust and feinted and slashed with surprising speed, and Fargo had his hands full just parrying the bowie knife. Robey's attack was so ferocious that Fargo was forced to give ground. From the corner of his eye he saw Grayson, Belinda, and Jimmy watching the clash with fear on their faces . . . fear for him, and fear for what might happen to them if Robey emerged victorious.

He didn't have time to worry about anything except the threat that was right in front of him. Robey was good, but he also got carried away by his emotions so that he grew careless at times. And he attacked with such enthusiasm that he began to tire himself out. Slowly but surely, Fargo turned the tide of battle. He was on the offensive now, forcing Robey back instead of the other way around.

Robey realized that things were no longer going his way. Fargo saw that unwelcome knowledge in the hardcase's eyes. Snarling curses, Robey found more strength somewhere inside him and renewed his attack with a fresh burst of ferocity.

But Fargo was a match for it. The Arkansas toothpick seemed to be everywhere at once, darting through the air with blinding speed, clanging against the bowie and turning it aside every time Robey tried a new thrust.

Desperate, Robey feinted with the knife and launched a kick at Fargo's groin. Fargo twisted and took the blow on his thigh, but it landed with enough power to stagger him. His foot slipped on something and he lost his balance.

Robey bellowed in triumph and drove forward, sweeping the bowie toward Fargo's chest. Another split second and the blade would be buried in Fargo's heart.

But Fargo didn't try to stay upright. He went over backward instead, letting his own momentum carry him away from the bowie. The razor-sharp tip of the knife raked a fiery line across his chest but didn't penetrate. As Fargo went down he drove the heel of his right boot against Robey's left knee. Bone shattered and Robey shrieked in pain. With the leg no longer able to support his weight, he toppled forward like a redwood tree falling in the forest.

Fargo was waiting with the Arkansas toothpick.

He drove the blade into Robey's chest. The hardcase's own weight assured that the toothpick went in all the way to the hilt. Robey gasped, his eyes widening in agony. The bowie slipped out of his suddenly nerveless fingers and clattered on the floor.

Fargo didn't let up on the pressure with the toothpick until Robey sighed and all the life went out of his eyes.

Then Fargo rolled the corpse off of him. Breathing hard from the exertion of the deadly battle, Fargo climbed to his feet. A grim smile touched his lips as he saw what had caused him to slip a moment earlier—a small puddle of blood that had come from Robey's broken nose.

He bent down and wiped the gore from his blade on the dead man's shirt. Then he faced Robey's friends and said, "I'm sorry I had to kill him. He started it, though."

"That's a damn lie," one of the men said. He pointed at Jimmy. "It was all that dummy's fault, and you're a damn murderer, Fargo. We'll have the law on you."

"Go ahead," Fargo told him. "Try it. But I don't think Hiram Stoddard will be very happy about you getting the law mixed up in his business."

He knew by the looks on their faces that his shot had found its mark. They were working for Stoddard, all right, and after having his men try to kidnap Belinda back in Los Angeles, as well as making the attempt on Fargo's life, it was true that Stoddard wouldn't want the authorities involved. He had too much to lose if the truth came out.

"You ain't seen the last of us," the man blustered.

Fargo sheathed the toothpick. "I'll keep that in mind," he said. "Maybe the next time I see you it'll be over the barrel of my Colt. For now, why don't you get the hell out of here?"

"What about him?" The man pointed at Robey's body.

"Take him with you," Fargo said. "I'm sure the proprietor of this cantina doesn't want him stinking up the place."

A couple of the men grabbed hold of the corpse by its legs and hauled it out of the cantina. The other hardcase followed them out, casting a murderous look in Fargo's direction as he did so.

From the table, Sandy said, "If you ask me, we'd best all stick together and sleep in the stable with the coach and the horses tonight, and take turns standin' guard to boot."

Fargo nodded. "Sounds like a good idea to me."

In the morning, they would resume their trip up the coast, which so far had proven to be a journey to violence.

That is, if they lived that long.

6

Not all the missions founded seventy to eighty years earlier by Father Junípero Sérra and other Franciscan friars were still being used. The Church no longer even owned all of the properties. Some, such as San Fernando, which the stagecoach had passed earlier that day, had fallen into disrepair.

San Buenaventura had fared better than most. Services were still held there, and the fields and orchards surrounding the mission still produced a bountiful harvest. The scent of blossoms on the fruit trees came faintly to Fargo's nose as he stood at the window of the hayloft in the stable, helping to mask the pungent animal smells from below.

Night had fallen, bringing a welcome hint of coolness to the air as well. Fargo was standing the first watch. He and Sandy and Grayson had drawn lots to determine the order of their shifts. Jimmy had volunteered to take a turn as well, but Sandy had convinced him to get a good night's sleep.

"We got to have them fresh horses, and it's up to you take care of 'em, son," Sandy had told the young man. "So you need to be fresh, too."

That had worked. Jimmy had agreed without taking offense. Fargo liked the youngster, and from what he had seen so far, Jimmy was a dependable, hard worker, but he didn't want to trust their lives to his vigilance.

Grayson had the second watch, and Sandy would finish off the night with the last shift. But for now, all of Fargo's senses were honed to high levels of alertness.

The night had been quiet and peaceful so far. Fargo stood far enough back from the window so that nobody could take a potshot at him from outside, but close enough to catch some of the breeze. He could see the stagecoach parked below. Anyone who tried to meddle with it would get a warm welcome from the big Sharps Fargo had tucked under his arm.

All the horses were in stalls down below. Another stall had been cleaned out so that Grayson, Sandy, and Jimmy could spread bedrolls there. Despite being something of a tenderfoot, Grayson hadn't complained about the arrangement.

"I grew up poor," he explained. "I've slept in worse places before this."

Belinda had been given the hostler's bunk in the tack room. With the graciousness of his people, the old-timer had surrendered the bunk without hesitation and tried to refuse any payment for his sacrifice, but Grayson had insisted on paying him. The old man had taken the gold coin Grayson gave him and wandered off, intent on finding a jug or a woman, or both.

Fargo was weary after a long day of riding, but he had no trouble staying awake. He had trained himself to be able to do that even when he was tired, because often his life had depended on it.

So he was a little surprised by the soft footstep behind him, but not by the fact that he heard it.

He whirled, every sense alert, every muscle tensed for action. His right hand dropped to the butt of the

Colt, ready to draw the weapon and fire in the blink of an eye.

The dark figure coming toward him stopped short. Fargo heard a startled gasp as the shape drew back a step.

"Belinda," he said, his voice little more than a whisper, "what are you doing up here?"

She had recoiled from the sudden violence of his reaction, but now she came forward again so that he could make out her face and figure in the light from the moon and stars. "I . . . I couldn't sleep," she said.

"So you thought you'd wander around in the dark for a while and maybe get yourself shot?"

She must have taken offense at the tone of rebuke in his voice, because she said, "You don't have to be like that about it. I just thought I'd come up here and keep you company for a while."

"I don't need to be kept company," Fargo said. "I'm supposed to be standing guard."

"Well, if I'm just going to be an annoyance . . ." Her voice was edgy with anger now.

Fargo knew the thing to do was to let her be angry. Let her go back down to the tack room.

If she was already having trouble sleeping, though, chances were she wouldn't be able to doze off now. She would nurse her hurt feelings, and that would keep her awake.

So he said, "No, stay. Truth is, I wouldn't mind having some company for a little while."

At that moment, one of the men below—Fargo thought it was Sandy—let out with a long, thunderous snore. That had been happening, off and on, all night. Fargo couldn't help but chuckle at the woeful tone in Belinda's voice as she said, "Good, because the tack room is right on the other side of where Mr. Stevens is sleeping, and that wall isn't very thick." She stepped closer and drew in a deep breath. "The night air smells wonderful."

"It's pretty nice," Fargo agreed. "There's a pile of hay over there if you want to sit down."

"No, this is all right. There might be . . . uh . . . bugs in that hay."

"Or rats," Fargo said.

Belinda shuddered and moved even closer to him.

"Rats?" she said, with worry in her voice.

"Don't worry. You'll hear them rustling around, if any of them are close by."

"Oh, that makes me feel *much* better." She was close beside him now, only inches away, her shoulder almost brushing his. "No one's tried to bother the coach, have they?"

Fargo shook his head. "No, it's been mighty peaceful tonight."

"Except for the part where you killed a man."

"Well," he said, "there was that."

"I . . . I never saw a man die before."

"The frontier's a pretty rugged place," Fargo said. "Maybe you should have stayed back east. Where do you and your father live when he's not running his stage lines?"

"St. Louis," she said. "And he didn't want to bring me. I insisted. I went with him to Texas when he was working there, and I thought California couldn't be any worse than that."

"It's not. But if you didn't run into any trouble in Texas, you were lucky."

"Actually, Father clashed with Mr. Stoddard there, too," Belinda said. "But it never got as far as violence. I suppose that must have been the last straw. Mr. Stoddard must have decided that Father would never get the best of him again, no matter what it took." She laid a hand on Fargo's arm. "There'll be

62

more danger before we get to San Francisco, won't there?"

"I reckon you can count on that," he told her.

She stood there beside him for several moments, silent in thought. Then she turned to him and said, "Since we don't know what's going to happen in the future, I'm not going to wait to do this."

She slid an arm around his neck, came up on her toes, and pressed her mouth to his.

He wasn't all that surprised by the kiss. He had seen in Belinda's eyes that she was attracted to him. And even though he didn't really need a distraction like this while he was standing guard, he couldn't bring himself to push her away. His right arm was free, since he was holding the Sharps in his left hand now, so he slipped it around her waist and urged her against him. Her body felt good as it molded to his, and her mouth tasted hot and sweet.

When she finally broke the kiss, she whispered, "Skye, we could put that pile of hay to good use."

The idea was mighty tempting. Ideas that involved piles of hay and beautiful, willing young women in the heat of night usually were.

But Fargo shook his head. He had to remain alert until the end of his watch, and anyway, Belinda's father was sleeping just below, along with Sandy and Jimmy. Nobody had ever accused him of being the soul of discretion, Fargo thought as he smiled to himself, but he had to draw the line somewhere.

"Maybe another time and place," he told her.

"But you said there was going to be more danger along the way," she argued. "Something could happen to one of us, or both of us. We might never get another chance to be together like this."

"Then that would be a mighty big shame. But it still doesn't mean *this* is the right time and place."

She moved back a little so that her face was in shadow, so he couldn't see her pout. He could hear it in her voice, though, as she said, "You just don't want me."

"I wouldn't say that," he told her. And if she could feel the stiffness inside his buckskin trousers right now, neither would she.

She might have argued some more, but at that moment Fargo tensed and lifted a hand. "Shhh," he said.

She talked anyway, whispering, "Is something wrong?"

He had seen something from the corner of his eye, and he wasn't quite sure what it was. Turning so that he faced the window, he peered out into the night.

The view from here was out over the yard in front of the stable and the cantina next door. A couple of hundred yards distant stood the old mission. Fargo had no trouble making out the long sanctuary with the sturdy bell tower located at the front of it. Beyond the mission, past the fields and the orchards, he saw the sparkle of moonlight on the endlessly rolling waters of the Pacific. On a quiet night such as this, the sound of the surf could be heard without much trouble.

Fargo leaned forward as he saw a light moving at the mission. "There it is again," he said, whispering even though he knew perfectly well that whoever was responsible for the light couldn't hear him at this distance.

"What are you talking about?" Belinda said. "That's just someone walking around with a lantern over there, isn't it?"

The light was a faint, shapeless glow. Fargo didn't think it came from a lantern. It was too vague for that. And something else wasn't quite right about it. . . .

"A few seconds ago, when I first saw the light, it was up in that bell tower," he said. "A man wouldn't have had enough time to climb all the way down and come outside."

That was where the light was now, moving along the front of the mission. Fargo blinked as it disappeared. Then, without warning, it reappeared, this time at the top of the bell tower again.

Belinda had seen it, too. She said, "Oh, my goodness. How did it do that?"

Fargo could only shake his head. "I don't know." As they stood there and watched, the light faded from sight bit by bit, until it was gone and didn't come back.

Fargo had always been one to trust the evidence of his own eyes, but right now he doubted what he had just seen. Belinda must have felt the same way, because she said, "That can't be, Skye. It just can't."

"We both saw it, so I reckon it has to be, whether we can explain it or not." His voice held a touch of dry humor as he added, "Unless we both had more tequila to drink at supper than I remember us having."

"That . . . whatever it was . . . has made me rather nervous. I don't think I want to go back down to the tack room alone. Do you mind if I stay up here with you until your watch is over?"

"You may be a mite tired in the morning, but it's all right with me," Fargo told her.

"Maybe I'll stretch out on that pile of hay after all."

Fargo thought at first that she might be about to try to seduce him again, but with a slight rustling of the hay she lay down, and within a few minutes, he heard her deep, regular breathing and knew she was asleep. She hadn't been so disturbed by the mysterious light that weariness hadn't been able to claim her.

He was in no danger of dozing off, though. Fargo was sure of that as he stared with narrowed eyes at the distant mission.

*　　*　　*

He let Belinda sleep until it was time to wake her father to take his turn on guard duty. Fargo roused her from slumber first, telling her that she needed to return to the tack room while Grayson was still asleep.

She stretched and said in a sleepy murmur, "I had the strangest dream, Skye. I dreamed there was this odd light moving around the mission. . . ." Her voice trailed off as she sat up. "It wasn't a dream, was it?"

"No, I saw it, too," Fargo told her. "And I don't have any more idea what it was now than I did then."

She shook her head. "I'm still glad I came up here, mystery lights and all. Glad I got a chance to tell you how I feel about you. I just wish . . ."

"Another time," Fargo said.

"Soon?"

"Soon," he promised with a smile.

He took her hand and helped her to her feet. She brushed hay off the skirt of her traveling outfit. "That was more comfortable than I thought it would be. And I don't seem to have been bothered by bugs . . . or rats."

Fargo took a last, quick look around from the loft window, then followed Belinda down the ladder. She gave him a hug and retreated to the tack room, easing the door shut behind her. Fargo went over to Grayson's bedroll and knelt beside him.

"Huh? What?" Grayson exclaimed as Fargo gave his shoulder a light shake. "Mr. Fargo! What is it?"

Fargo could tell by the man's confusion that he had been sleeping soundly. "Your turn to stand guard, Mr. Grayson," he said. "You sure you're up to it?"

Grayson sat up and rubbed his eyes with his fists. "Yes, I'm fine," he said in a half whisper so he wouldn't disturb Sandy and Jimmy. He got to his feet and followed Fargo over to the ladder.

Fargo pressed the Sharps into his hand. "Ever use one of these before?"

"As a matter of fact, I have. They've got a kick like a Missouri mule, don't they?"

Fargo smiled. "Yes, but you don't have to worry about precise aim. Hit a man anywhere with a shot from one of these and he's going to be knocked off his feet."

Fargo gave Grayson some extra rounds for the carbine, then waited until the man had climbed to the loft before heading for his own bedroll. He fell asleep a short time later, not bothered by Sandy's snoring, the small noises made by the horses as they shifted around in their stalls, or the memory of that mysterious light at the mission.

The rest of the night passed without any trouble. The next morning, while Sandy and Jimmy were tending to the horses, Fargo asked Belinda, "Sleep well?"

"Surprisingly well," she said. With a smile, she added, "After a certain point, anyway."

They ate breakfast at the cantina, then got ready to hit the trail again. Fargo left saddling the Ovaro until last. When he went into the stable he found the hostler combing the big black-and-white stallion.

"He must like you," Fargo said. "He won't let just anybody come around him. The big fella's been known to take a bite out of a man's hide if he doesn't take a liking to him."

"The horse knows that I have only admiration for him, senor," the old-timer said as he stroked the Ovaro's nose. "No one can see the truth in a person's heart more clearly than a *caballo*."

Fargo liked the hostler and sensed that the old man was trustworthy, so he ventured a question. "I saw something a mite odd over at the mission last night. I was wondering if you might know what it was."

"Was it a light, senor?"

Fargo frowned, a little surprised by the hostler's question. "As a matter of fact, it was."

The old man nodded. "*Sí*, of course. What you saw was Father Tomás, Senor Fargo."

"You mean one of the padres from the mission? I wasn't even sure if it was still being used as a church." Fargo shook his head. "But what I saw couldn't have been a priest. The light didn't really look like a lantern. And it was up in the bell tower, then on the ground, then back up in the bell tower, all in a matter of a minute or so."

"*Sí, señor.* Father Tomás."

Fargo was starting to get a mite impatient and frustrated. "I never saw a priest who could fly," he said, "and that's what it would take to make that light jump around like that. Anyway, like I told you, it didn't look like a lantern."

The hostler shook his head. "No, senor, it was not a lantern. Like *I* told *you*, the light was Father Tomás himself."

"But how—"

"And of course he can fly," the old man said. "He is, after all, a ghost."

7

For a moment, all Fargo could do was stare at the hostler. The old man didn't seem to be trying to make a joke at his expense. The lined, weathered, nut brown face was as serious as it could be.

"A ghost?" Fargo finally said.

"*Sí, señor.* He seeks the lost treasure of San Buenaventura."

"Lost treasure," Fargo repeated. He was starting to suspect that the old man was just spinning a yarn. A local folk tale, at best.

"*Sí.* Forty years ago, Father Tomás received word that a notorious pirate, an Argentinean devil named Bouchard, who raided along this coast and caused much sorrow and weeping, was going to sail to San Buenaventura and loot it of all its treasures. Father Tomás feared not only for the Church's holy vessels and icons but also for the safety of his flock, at that time mostly Indians. So he had them gather up everything of any value in the mission and took them all into the hills, where the treasure was hidden in a cave." The hostler's bony shoulders rose and fell in a shrug. "Of course, the pirate Bouchard did not sack the mission. In fact, he did not even stop at San Buenaventura but instead sailed on past as if the devil had wings, bent on mischief elsewhere, no doubt."

"Let me guess," Fargo said. "When Father Tomás went back to the cave to retrieve the treasure he had hidden, it was gone."

"Not all of it, senor. Only one bag. But that bag contained the most priceless items from the church."

Fargo nodded. He was well aware of how the brown-robed padres who had colonized the Southwest for Spain had used gold and silver mined by their Indian parishioners to craft chalices, picture frames, candlesticks, and other items that were worth a fortune.

"Father Tomás was brokenhearted that a member of his flock would stoop to stealing from the Church," the old-timer went on. "It is said that he died not long afterward from that broken heart. Soon after that, his ghost appeared, and everyone knew why. The padre's spirit is restless. It cannot know peace until it has found the treasure that was lost while he was trying to save it from the pirates."

Fargo glanced through the open doors of the stable and saw that one of the teams was hitched to the stagecoach and the other horses had been roped together by Jimmy, who was now on his own mount holding the lead rope. Sandy held the door of the coach open so that Grayson and Belinda, the only passengers, could climb inside. They would all be ready to go in another minute or two.

The hostler's story hadn't really answered Fargo's question about the mysterious light at the mission, but it was a good yarn nonetheless, the Trailsman thought. He just didn't believe it, because he didn't believe in ghosts. He had seen some mighty strange things in his life, but sooner or later, they all had a reasonable explanation.

He took a coin from his pocket and pressed it in the old man's hand. "I'm obliged, amigo," he said. "For your hospitality and your friendship."

"*De nada, señor.* You are welcome in the village of Ventura anytime."

Fargo swung up on the stallion and rode out of the stable, turning in the saddle to lift a hand in farewell to the old Mexican. Sandy slammed the coach door after Grayson and Belinda and climbed onto the driver's seat as Fargo rode over beside the big Concord.

"Ready to roll?" Fargo asked.

Sandy unwrapped the reins from the brake lever and nodded. "Ready as we're ever gonna be," he replied.

"Let's move out, then," Fargo said with a wave of his hand. He heeled the Ovaro into a trot and led the way.

But as he rode past the old mission, he couldn't help but glance at the bell tower and recall the mysterious light he had seen hovering in it. The old man's story about lost treasure and the ghost of a long-dead padre couldn't be true.

Could it?

The next stop along the coast on the Old Mission Trail was at Santa Barbara. The coach approached it around midday. This part of the journey had been easy. Although narrow and ungraded, the trail was simple to follow and ran along the flat coastal plain, with a range of low mountains rising to the east. Fargo loped along on the stallion about a hundred yards ahead of the coach. Down a drop-off to his left was the beach, with the surf crashing ashore as it had for untold centuries.

The growing settlement of Santa Barbara was sprawled along the shore just above the sea, where several wharves jutted out into the water. The mission, with its distinctive twin bell towers, was a mile or so to the east, looking a little like a European castle as it perched atop a small hill with the mountains in the background. The red tile roofs of the buildings shone brightly in the noontime sun.

Fargo reined the Ovaro to a halt in front of the first stable he came to. A heavyset man with a bulldog jaw and bright red side-whiskers came out of the barn and said, "Good day to ye, son. Somethin' I can do for you?"

Fargo gestured toward the approaching stagecoach. "We'd like to stop here and change teams if that's all right with you, mister. In fact, if you have any good fresh horses for sale, we might be able to work a deal."

A grin wreathed the man's pleasantly ugly face. "I'm always open to a little horse tradin'," he declared. "Seamus McPhee is my name."

Fargo introduced himself and reached down to shake hands. "I'm pleased to meet you, Mr. McPhee."

"What's a stagecoach doin' here, anyway?"

"Establishing a new stage line from Los Angeles to San Francisco," Fargo explained. "The owner and his daughter are in the coach."

McPhee put his hands on his broad hips. "Well, what do ye know about that? Ye don't think the fellow might be interested in havin' a stage station here in Santa Barbara, do ye?"

"I think Mr. Grayson would be very glad to talk to you about that," Fargo said. "Fact of the matter is, he's looking for men to operate stations and provide fresh teams for his coaches."

"Well, he's come to the right place, by Godfrey!"

The stopover at Santa Barbara went very well. Arthur Grayson and Seamus McPhee hit it off right away, and over lunch at a nearby tavern, they made arrangements for McPhee to operate the stage station here and provide horses for the line. He would be able to continue his livery stable business at the same time, so it was a good deal for the Irishman. He also sold a team of fresh horses to Grayson for the rest of the run up the coast.

The afternoon was spent covering the distance between Santa Barbara and Santa Inés. The trail was rough and curved slightly to the east, twisting in and out among the foothills as the mountains began to crowd in on the sea. Once it was through the hills, the stagecoach traveled along a fertile valley between two ranges of peaks. Fargo could no longer see or hear the Pacific Ocean, but he knew it was there, just beyond the heavily wooded mountains to the west.

They reached Santa Inés late in the afternoon. The neighboring village of Los Olivos was tiny compared to Santa Barbara, which, as one of the best ports along this stretch of coast, was developing into a good-sized settlement. Los Olivos, on the other hand, was nothing more than a tavern, a blacksmith shop, and a few huts.

"This is where we're going to have to spend the night?" Belinda asked from the window of the coach when the vehicle had rocked to a stop.

Fargo nodded. "It's not much, but better than nothing, I reckon."

Belinda didn't look like she was convinced of that.

Fargo dismounted and went into the tavern, which was a long, low building with a thatched roof. Outside, the sun had almost set, and inside, the tavern was already dim and smoky. This valley was farming rather than ranching country, and the men at the bar wore rough white shirts and trousers of homespun cotton. Battered straw hats were shoved to the backs of their heads.

The customers were all of Mexican descent, but the big man behind the bar was blond and blue-eyed, with a bald head and a jutting beard. A fat belly swelled the front of the dingy apron he wore. His arms and shoulders were laden with thick slabs of muscle. He scowled at Fargo and asked, "What do you want, mister?"

His accent was Swedish, Fargo thought, recognizing it because he had been to Minnesota a time or two, and yet the words had an odd lilt to them. Fargo figured out why as the proprietor turned his head to some of the men at the bar and spoke to them in rapid, fluent Spanish. The man's accent was a mixture of influences from both languages.

"I'm traveling with some folks who need a place to stay for the night, as well as some food," Fargo said, ignoring for the moment his instinctive dislike of the man.

The proprietor jerked a blunt thumb over his shoulder. "I got a couple o' rooms out back you can rent," he said. "Cost you dear, though. There ain't another place to stay in the valley unless you want to camp by the old trail."

For a moment Fargo gave that thought some serious consideration. He didn't like this hombre, and the place looked none too clean. But, as he had told Belinda already, he supposed it was better than nothing.

"I'll tell the others and let them decide," he said with a nod.

"Don't blame me if some other pilgrims come along and rent them rooms while you're makin' up your mind."

Fargo ignored the surly comment. The trail was almost deserted, so he didn't think there was much chance of someone renting the rooms out from under them.

He went outside and explained the situation to Grayson and Belinda, who had climbed out of the coach. Grayson looked at his daughter and asked, "What do you think?"

Belinda turned to Fargo. "Is it safe here, Skye?"

"Safe enough. Probably not very comfortable, though."

She laughed. "We spent last night in a stable, remember?"

"You've got a point there," Fargo agreed with a smile.

"All right, then," Grayson said. "Tell the man we'll take the rooms. Belinda can have one of them and the rest of us will share the other one. Do we need to stand watch again, like we did last night?"

"Wouldn't be a bad idea," Fargo said. "I haven't seen any sign of Stoddard's men all day, but I'd be willing to bet they're not far off, just waiting for a chance to strike at us again."

Fargo went back inside, followed by Grayson and Belinda, while Sandy and Jimmy tended to the horses. Fargo said to the big blond man behind the bar, "We'll rent those rooms."

The man grunted. "Figured you would." He turned his head and bellowed, "Angie!"

A girl came through a door that led to the rear of the tavern. She wore an old dress that had been patched in several places, as well as an apron that had once been white but now was as gray as the one the owner wore. She kept her head down so that her thick blond hair hung around her face, concealing her features.

"You get them rooms cleaned up like I told you?" the proprietor asked in a harsh voice.

The girl's reply was so soft Fargo had trouble hearing it. "Yes, sir."

"Got the stew cookin'?" The man's tone was still sharp and impatient.

"Yes, sir."

"Good. We got folks stayin' the night. You dish up some food for 'em—you hear me? And don't waste any time doin' it. Rattle them lazy bones o' yours!"

The girl turned to retreat into the back of the tavern. Fargo wasn't sure how old she was—fifteen or sixteen, he guessed, maybe a little older—but she moved like she had the weight of decades on her. He had seen the way she flinched when the man roared at her. Fargo's eyes narrowed as he thought about that.

He was starting to dislike the fella behind the bar more and more.

Grayson and Belinda took seats at a rough-hewn table. Fargo asked the owner, "You have any beer?"

"*Cerveza?* Sure. Four bits a glass."

"Steep," Fargo commented.

"Where else are you gonna—"

"Get any around here, I know," Fargo broke in. He dropped a coin on the bar, hoping that the beer would be better than the owner's attitude.

It wasn't.

He was still sipping the watery, bitter brew when Sandy and Jimmy came in and joined him at the bar. "We made a deal with the blacksmith," Sandy told Fargo. "He's got a corral, where we're keepin' the horses tonight. Stage is parked right beside it."

Fargo nodded. "That sounds like the best we can do. Which seems to be a pretty common state of affairs around here, by the way."

"Is that beer you're drinkin'?" Sandy asked as he pointed at the cup in Fargo's hand.

"Sort of. The closest thing to it you're going to find in Los Olivos, anyway."

Sandy signaled for the big blond man to bring him

a cup, and when he had tried the beer, he smacked his lips, made a face, and said, "You weren't joshin', were you, Fargo?"

The girl emerged from the back, carrying a platter with several bowls of stew on it. The smell that came from the bowls was the first good thing Fargo had encountered in this place. The appetizing aroma was laden with spices and wild onions and roasted meat.

"Who's that?" Jimmy asked.

Fargo turned to look at the young man and saw that Jimmy was staring at the girl. "She works here. The owner's daughter or niece or something like that, more than likely," Fargo explained. He didn't add that the man talked to her like she was some sort of slave.

"She sure is pretty," Jimmy breathed with a note of awestruck wonder in his voice.

Fargo tried not to frown. To him the girl seemed to be on the scrawny side, and he still hadn't seen her face because of the way her hair hung over it. Jimmy was entranced by her, though.

Sandy saw the same thing and said to the young man, "Better steer clear of her, boy. You don't want her pa comin' after you with a shotgun. Anyway"—he glanced at the table where Belinda was sitting and lowered his voice so she wouldn't hear—"females is nothin' but trouble. Sure, they're soft and purty and mighty good for warmin' a man's feet on a cold night, but if you go to bein' nice to 'em, 'fore you know it they're askin' you to *do* things, like don't track mud in the house and take your spurs off 'fore you sit at the table and . . . and take a bath, for God's sake! Hell, there's all kinds o' things they want you to do, and the worst of it is, half the time they won't even *tell* you what they want."

Jimmy looked confused. "Then how are you supposed to know what to do?"

"That there's one o' the great unsolved mysteries o' the universe, son. You just have to guess. But you damn well better guess right, 'cause you'll be in a whole heap o' trouble if you don't." Sandy put a hand on the youngster's shoulder. "Now have you learned anythin' from what I just told you?"

Jimmy bobbed his head. "Yes, sir."

"What? What did you learn?"

But the girl was moving past the end of the bar, going back into the kitchen to fetch more bowls of stew, and Jimmy was already gazing at her again with longing in his eyes, Sandy's words forgotten.

"Gee, she sure is pretty," he said.

Sandy muttered, raked his fingers through his beard, and downed the rest of his beer, grimacing as he did so.

The stew tasted as good as it smelled. The five travelers gathered around the table and ate several bowls apiece, even Belinda. By the time they were finished, it was fully dark outside, and Belinda was yawning.

"I think I'd like to go ahead and turn in," she said.

Fargo nodded. He stood up and went over to the bar. "The lady is going to her room," he told the proprietor.

The man grunted. "Fine with me, soon as you pay up." He named a price.

Fargo thought the amount was outrageous, but Grayson had given him money to pay for expenses. He passed over the coins, and after the owner had bitten each of them to make sure they were good, he shouted again, "Angie!"

The girl hurried out from the back. The sleeves of her dress were pushed up, and her hands and forearms were wet. She had been washing dishes in the kitchen, Fargo thought.

"Take the lady back and show her to her room," the proprietor ordered.

Angie nodded and turned toward the table where Belinda still sat with her father, Sandy, and Jimmy.

"Wait just a damned minute!" the blond man roared. He reached over the bar and grabbed the girl's arm. Fargo frowned as he saw the fingers dig into the flesh.

The man shook Angie and went on. "That there's a lady, not a stupid little bitch like you! Go dry your hands first!" He shoved her toward the door. "I swear, you ain't got a lick o' sense in that head o' yours."

Tight-lipped with anger, Fargo said, "No call to treat the girl like that, mister."

The man stared at him in surprise. "No call?" he repeated. "No call? Mister, I'll treat her any damn way I please! This is my place, and I won't be told what I can or can't do!"

With that, he stepped out from behind the bar. The girl lunged for the door, but he caught hold of her before she could reach it. He jerked her around with his left hand and brought the right around in a vicious slap that cracked across her face, knocking her head to the side. Stunned, she went to one knee and would have fallen all the way to the floor if not for the cruel grip he still maintained on her arm.

With a defiant glare at Fargo, the man went on. "I'll thrash her within an inch of her worthless life if that's what I want to do!"

Fargo ignored the obvious challenge for the moment. He was busy looking down at the girl, whose head drooped to the side now so that her hair no longer covered all of her face. He saw the ugly puckered scar that covered her left cheek and understood why she kept her head down all the time. She didn't want people staring at the damage that had been done to her sometime in the past, probably by a fire.

Taking his time about it, Fargo lifted his gaze so that it met that of the proprietor. In a quiet voice, he asked, "What's your name, mister?"

The man was taken aback by that unexpected question, but he answered, "Matthias Jarlberg, if it's any o' your business."

"Oh, it's my business," Fargo said. "I'd like to know who it is I'm about to beat the hell out of."

8

The few farmers who remained in the tavern began sidling toward the door, not wasting any time about it as they did so. A couple of them cast nervous glances back over their shoulders, as if they knew a terrible storm was about to break.

Fargo didn't care. He was so mad that he would saddle that storm and ride it until it played out.

Jarlberg stared at Fargo for a moment before he demanded, "What did you just say to me, mister?"

"You heard me," Fargo snapped. "I'm going to beat the hell out of you and see how you like it for a change."

"All because o' the way I treat this ignorant little slut? What in blazes does she mean to you?" A canny look came into the man's piggish little eyes. "If you're sweet on her, you can have her for the night. Won't cost you much, on account of she's ugly—"

Jimmy stood up at the table and said, "Don't you talk like that about her, mister! Don't you say things like that!"

"Lord, now the damn half-wit's startin' in on me," Jarlberg muttered.

"You're just digging yourself a deeper hole," Fargo said.

Jarlberg glanced down at the revolver on Fargo's

hip. He licked his lips. "I ain't no gunfighter. I see you carry a big pigsticker, too, and I ain't no good with one of them, neither."

"Don't worry," Fargo told him. "Shooting you or carving you up wouldn't be near as satisfying as pounding you with my fists."

"All right, all right!" Jarlberg held up his hands in surrender. "What do you want me to do, apologize to her?"

"That'd be a start."

"Fine." Scowling and muttering, Jarlberg turned to Angie. She drew in a sharp, nervous breath and sidled backward as he took a step toward her. "Take it easy. I'm just sayin' that I'm sorry for the way I treated you, gal. I won't do it no more." He glanced over his shoulder at Fargo. "Is that good enough?"

Fargo gave a curt nod. "I reckon." He started to turn back toward the table where the others were.

Even before Jimmy yelled "Mr. Fargo, look out!" he sensed the threatening movement behind him. A quick twist of his body showed Jarlberg lunging at him. The man had grabbed a tequila bottle from the bar. He swept it at Fargo's head in a vicious blow.

Fargo was expecting just such a treacherous move. He hadn't believed Jarlberg's insincere apology for a second. His own reaction was swift as lightning. He ducked so that the bottle passed over his head, although it came close enough to clip his hat and send it sailing. Fargo lowered his head even more and charged forward, slamming into Jarlberg.

It was a little like tackling a mountain, but the man was off balance and Fargo put all his power into the pile-driving lunge. Jarlberg grunted as Fargo shoved him backward. The grunt turned into a yell of pain as his back crashed into the bar.

The bar swayed under the impact but didn't tip over.

Jarlberg was bent over the hardwood. Grimacing in pain, he dropped the bottle and hammered both fists against Fargo's back. Fargo let go and stepped back. His ribs ached a little from the clublike blows, but he could tell that Jarlberg hadn't done any real damage.

Panting as he tried to catch his breath, Jarlberg said, "I'll kill you . . . you bastard." Then he roared and came at Fargo.

The Trailsman met the attack with a chopping left and then a hard overhand right, both of which landed with solid thuds against Jarlberg's jaw. Jarlberg smashed a right to Fargo's midsection, then followed it with a looping left that caught Fargo in the chest. Fargo was rocked back by the punches, but he caught himself and hooked a left and a right to Jarlberg's belly.

Despite looking fat, the man was mostly muscle. Punching him in the stomach was like hitting a stone wall. Fargo tried to slip an uppercut to the chin past Jarlberg's guard, but he parried the blow. The next instant a punch exploded in Fargo's face, sending him flying backward. Jarlberg was faster than he looked.

Fargo caught himself on one of the tables. As Jarlberg rushed him, Fargo brought a foot up and planted it in Jarlberg's stomach. A hard shove sent the man stumbling against the bar again.

From the corner of his eye Fargo caught a glimpse of his companions watching the battle with anxious expressions on their faces. The girl, Angie, had retreated all the way to the door leading into the rear of the tavern, but she didn't disappear through it. Instead she stood there with one hand clutching the door, waiting to see what the outcome was going to be. Her head was tilted so that her hair once again covered the scarred left side of her face, but she watched out of her bright blue right eye.

Bellowing like a bull, Jarlberg charged again. Fargo

met him head-on, and for a long moment, the two men stood toe-to-toe, slugging away at each other, dishing out punishment and receiving it in kind. Fargo concentrated his blows on Jarlberg's face and head, knowing it wouldn't do any good to go after his body, coated with thick layers of muscle as it was. Jarlberg's punches were wilder, more flailing, and although some of them got through, Fargo was able to parry and avoid many of them.

Slowly, Fargo's more efficient style of fighting began to have an effect. Jarlberg's face was bloody from the several cuts that Fargo's flashing fists had doled out. His mouth was a crimson mess, and both eyes were beginning to swell shut. His looping overhand punches were slower now and had less strength behind them. Fargo was able to turn them aside without much trouble and counterpunch. Jarlberg's arms finally dropped, and he reeled backward.

Fargo bored in, snapping rights and lefts that splattered more blood from his opponent's face. Jarlberg slumped against the bar. Fargo hit him with a solid right, then stepped back as he saw Jarlberg's eyes roll up in their sockets. Out cold, the man pitched forward to land on the floor with a thunderous crash.

In the echoing silence that followed that collapse, Sandy said, "You beat the hell out of him, all right, Fargo. I thought for a second there you was gonna kill the son of a bitch."

Fargo's chest heaved. He ached all over from the pounding Jarlberg had given him, and his own mouth was bleeding a little. But as he wiped away the blood, he nodded and said, "For a second there, I thought about it."

His four companions came over to him, and Grayson asked, "Are you all right?"

"I'll be a mite stiff and sore in the morning, I expect," Fargo admitted. "But I'm fine. Somehow, though, I don't think we'll be welcome to spend the night here after all."

Belinda shuddered. "I wouldn't want to spend the night under the roof of an animal like him. I'd rather sleep in the stagecoach."

"I reckon that's what you'll have to do," Fargo said. "We can spread a couple of bedrolls underneath it, and one man can sleep on top. It won't be comfortable, but it's the best we can do."

From the open doorway of the tavern, a voice said, "No, senor, it is not."

Fargo looked around to see several of the farmers who had been at the bar earlier. One of them had spoken.

The man went on. "Our homes are not much, but you and your amigos are welcome to share them, senor. Senor Jarlberg is a terrible man. None of us likes him. He charges too much and calls us names. What you have given him tonight, he has had coming for a long time."

Another of the farmers added, "Please, senor, you would honor us by accepting our hospitality."

Fargo looked at the others. "What do you think?"

"I think it's a very generous offer," Grayson said, "and we should accept it." Belinda nodded.

"Go ahead," Sandy said. "Me and Jimmy will stay and guard the coach and the horses."

Fargo had been worried about that very thing, but now he nodded and said to the farmers, "All right, you've got a deal." He bent over and reached in the pocket of Jarlberg's apron, where the man had dropped the coins Fargo had given him earlier. "But by all rights, these ought to be yours."

He tossed the money to the farmers.

One more thing bothered Fargo. He turned to the

girl and asked, "Are you going to be all right once he wakes up?"

She nodded, catching her bottom lip between her teeth as she did so.

"You're sure?" Fargo insisted. "He won't take his anger out on you?"

She shook her head, clearly unwilling to speak.

Fargo had to accept her answers. He said, "All right, if you're sure." He picked up his hat and the Sharps, which he had placed on one of the tables, and ushered the others outside.

Sandy and Jimmy were going to sleep inside the coach with their rifles. Fargo, Grayson, and Belinda were escorted to the nearby homes of a couple of the farmers. Fargo stayed in one of the huts, Grayson and Belinda in the other. Their hosts left them alone for the night, doubling up with some of their friends.

Once he was alone, stretched out on a rope bunk with his boots and gun belt and buckskin shirt off, Fargo let out a low groan. Even though most of Jarlberg's punches had been wild, the ones that landed had felt like sledgehammers. Fargo knew he was lucky that his active life had given him the sort of iron constitution that enabled him to shake off such injuries in a hurry.

He dozed off and didn't know how long he had been asleep when a stealthy sound woke him. His Colt was on the floor right beside the bunk. Without making a sound, he dropped his hand to the gun and closed his fingers around the walnut grips.

"Skye?" Belinda whispered in the darkness.

Fargo wasn't surprised. He'd been halfway expecting her, in fact. He didn't have an ounce of vanity in him. He knew he couldn't have any woman he wanted. But at the same time, he was a man who recognized facts, and he was aware that plenty of women were attracted to him. Belinda had demonstrated the night before that she was one of them.

"Over here," he said.

She came to him as he sat up on the bunk. The farmer's hut had only a couple of windows, but they let in enough starlight for her to find her way around. She sat down beside him and said, "I've been thinking about you ever since last night, Skye."

"That was a mighty nice kiss, all right," Fargo admitted.

"Nice enough so that I want more. A lot more." She put a hand on his bare shoulder and let it caress his skin. "But I didn't know if I ought to come over here or not. You must be awfully sore after that fight."

"I'm all right," Fargo told her. "Your father's liable to wake up and worry if he finds you gone, though."

Belinda laughed. "He won't wake up. I told you he's a sound sleeper."

"In that case . . ."

Fargo turned toward her and took her in his arms, discovering as he did so that she was dressed only in a thin wrapper. Her flesh was soft and pliant under his hands as he drew her to him. Acting on instinct, they had no trouble finding each other's mouths, even in the dark.

In truth, Fargo was pretty bruised and sore from the battering. But he was also so aroused by Belinda's soft warmth and the sweet taste of her mouth that he forgot all about any aches and pains as he hugged and kissed her. He tugged on her so that she straddled his hips, settling her pelvis down against his. He still wore his buckskin trousers and she had on the flimsy robe, but they felt each other's heat and desire anyway. Belinda moaned into Fargo's mouth as she ground herself against his hardness.

She pulled her lips away from his and whispered, "We've got to . . . get rid of these clothes!" Her words were urgent with need.

She stripped her wrap off and tossed it aside. Fargo ran his hands over her body, loving the feel of her. He cupped her firm breasts and found the hard nipples with his thumbs. She clutched at his broad, muscular chest and leaned down to rain kisses on it.

Fargo let go of her as she continued sliding down his body, trailing hot kisses over his flat, hard stomach. Her hands hooked the waistband of his trousers and pulled. He raised his hips so that she could pull them off of him. His erect member sprang free. Its thick, impressive length jutted up from his groin. Belinda caught hold of it and rubbed the head against her cheek. With her other hand, she pushed his trousers down around his ankles.

The heat of her mouth was incredible as she closed her lips around his shaft. He leaned his head back against the wall as waves of pleasure cascaded through him. Either she had experience or a natural talent for what she was doing, and Fargo didn't care which it was. He was beyond caring about much of anything except the wonderful sensations her mouth bestowed on him.

With one hand, she pumped slowly on his shaft, while the other cupped the heavy sac at the base of his manhood. All the while, her lips and tongue continued their exquisite teasing. When at last she closed her lips, hollowed her cheeks, and sucked hard on him, it was all he could do not to let himself explode in her mouth. He wanted to delay his climax, though, until she was ready to share it.

When she raised her head from his groin, he put his hands under her arms and lifted her slender figure like she weighed little or nothing. Holding her above his throbbing hardness, he lowered her onto it, letting his shaft sink into her inch by inch. She gasped when he hit bottom, sheathed all the way inside her.

They stayed there like that for a long moment, luxuriating in their closeness. Then Fargo withdrew a little and surged up again, causing a delicious friction as he slid between the slick folds of her femininity. Belinda rocked her hips to meet his thrust. They fell into a rhythm, rocking and thrusting, that sent their shared arousal spiraling higher and higher.

Together, they climbed those heights until Fargo felt his culmination boiling up inside him. It was too strong to be denied. Thankfully, he didn't have to, because at that moment shudders began to ripple through Belinda's body and he knew she had reached her own climax. He drove hard up into her, burying his manhood to the deepest possible point, and let go, emptying himself into her.

A final spasm went through Belinda, and then she seemed to melt against him, the muscles that she had tensed as her climax swept over her all going soft and yielding. She rested her head on his shoulder. He felt her hot breath against his neck. Turning his head so that his lips nuzzled her ear, he stroked her back. Her heart beat strongly against his chest. He figured she could feel his heart beating as well.

When she had caught her breath enough to be able to speak again, she said, "Skye, that was . . . that was as good as I thought it would be. Hoped it would be. Every bit as good."

"Yes, it was," he agreed.

"I wish I could spend the rest of the night here, so

that we could do it again. Maybe even more than once."

"But it'll be dawn in an hour or so," Fargo said. The faint tinge of gray in the sky he could see through the window of the hut told him that.

"Yes. I'd better get back." She lifted her head and kissed him again. The urgency was gone now, but not the sensuous delight they both took in each other's lips.

After a few moments, she slipped out of his arms and picked up her robe from the floor. Wrapping it around her, she went to the door, eased it open, and went out, pausing only to glance back at him one last time. Because of the darkness, Fargo couldn't read the expression on her face. He hoped it was a satisfied one.

He lay back on the bunk and took several deep breaths. Now that Belinda was gone, he was beginning to feel those bruises again. But he smiled, knowing they didn't really amount to anything. In a day or two, it would be like he had never had that battle with Matthias Jarlberg.

Thinking about the tavern owner made Fargo frown. He sat up and swung his legs off the bunk, then stood and went to the door. From there he could see the long, low bulk of the tavern. The building was dark now, closed down for the night. He wondered what, if anything, was going on in there. A part of him worried that he shouldn't have left Angie there. There was no telling what Jarlberg might have done when he regained consciousness. He might have gone into an insane rage.

And yet, Angie ought to know him well enough to know whether or not she would be in danger, Fargo thought. She had seemed confident she would be all right—or at least as confident as someone could be whose spirit had been beaten down as Angie's was.

Fargo shook his head and went back to the bunk. The night was quiet, and within minutes he had dropped off to sleep, taking advantage of the time he had left before a new day began.

9

"I want to go with you."

The words were spoken in a quiet voice—so quiet that even Fargo's keen ears had a little trouble making them out. As usual, Angie's eyes were downcast as she made her request.

Fargo put his hand under her chin and brought it up, lifting her head so that she had to look at him. She used her right hand to push her hair back on that side, but left the hair on the left alone so that it obscured her burned cheek.

"What about Jarlberg?" Fargo asked.

She cast a nervous glance toward the tavern, which sat dark and silent in the gray dawn. "That's why I want to go with you," she said. "He—he's asleep now, but he swore he'd get even with you . . . and with me. I—I'm afraid of what he might do."

Fargo wasn't afraid of Jarlberg, but he could understand how this slip of a girl would be. Despite her confidence of the night before, fear had caught up to her and prompted her to slip out here while Fargo, Sandy, and Jimmy were getting the teams and the coach ready for another day of travel. Belinda and Grayson were still asleep in the farmer's hut.

"Please let her come with us, Mr. Fargo," Jimmy

put in from the back of the coach, where he had been securing the canvas cover over the boot after stowing away some of their gear. "That fella Mr. Jarlberg might go on a rampage. He's a bad man."

In his own way, Jimmy cut right to the heart of the matter. Fargo didn't trust Jarlberg. They had already seen plenty of evidence that the man mistreated Angie on a regular basis. Filled with rage and the desire for revenge, there was no telling what he might do.

Fargo looked at Angie. He didn't see any fresh bruises or other signs of violence on her. After the thrashing Fargo had given Jarlberg, he probably hadn't felt like dishing out any punishment to the girl the night before. But when he awoke this morning, that might be a different story.

"Who is he to you?" Fargo asked. "Any kin?"

She shook her head, making her hair move and giving him a glimpse of her scarred cheek. "No. He's no kin. He was a friend of my father. When the fever took my mother, and then my father died not long after, Mr. Jarlberg said he'd take me in and give me a place to live if I'd work for him. I—I didn't have anyplace else to go."

Fargo heard the bleak desperation in her voice and knew it must have been a terrible time for her. But despite the sympathy he felt for her, he wanted to know exactly what she had in mind.

"Where will you go if you come along with us?"

"You're bound for San Francisco, aren't you? I can get by in a big town like that. I'm a hard worker. And I ain't afraid of anything except . . ."

Her eyes darted toward the tavern.

"You don't have any relatives in San Francisco?"

"No, sir. But like I said, I can get by."

She would wind up in a Barbary Coast whorehouse, Fargo told himself. Even with that scarred cheek, she was young enough and pretty enough to last for a while, and she probably wasn't inexperienced. Jarlberg had talked like he'd rented her out to travelers before. But it would be a hell of a grim life, and probably a short one, too.

What did she have to look forward to here, though? Years of abuse at the hands of the brutish Jarlberg? Would that really be any better?

Fargo couldn't answer those questions, but he knew that if Angie left this place, at least she would have a chance, slim though it might be, for a better life. As he came to that realization, he nodded and said, "You can come with us."

She smiled. The expression was an awkward one, as if she hadn't had much practice at it. "Thank you, Mr. Fargo," she whispered.

"Go get your stuff, but be quiet about it. You don't want to wake him up."

"I can go with her," Jimmy volunteered.

"You stay right here, boy," Sandy told him. "No offense, but them big clodhoppers o' yours make enough noise to wake the dead when you go to trompin' around."

"That's all right," Angie said. "I'll be right back."

Like a shadow, she flitted off toward the tavern and disappeared inside.

Sandy came over to the Trailsman with a frown on his face. "You sure this is a good idea, Fargo?" he asked. "When that fella Jarlberg finds out the gal's gone, he's liable to come after us and cause us even more trouble."

"I thought about that," Fargo admitted, "but I don't think he'll do it. That would mean leaving the tavern, and I'm not sure he'd trust the folks around here not to break in and help themselves while he's gone. He's bound to know that he's not well liked. He might even be afraid that they'd burn the place down if he left."

Sandy scratched at his beard. "Yeah, could be. Anyway, I don't reckon we can leave the poor little gal. No tellin' what that Scandahoovian bastard might do to her if we did." He shook his head. "I ain't that fond o' havin' another of her species along for the ride, though. Sooner or later, them blasted females always mean trouble."

Fargo chuckled and went to saddle the Ovaro. He kept an ear out for sounds of trouble from the tavern, just in case Jarlberg woke up before Angie could gather her few belongings and leave.

The place was still quiet as she stole out of it a few minutes later and hurried over to the coach. She carried a small carpetbag. Jimmy had unfastened the cover over the boot again and pulled it back. He took the bag from her and placed it inside.

"There you go," he told her with a shy smile. "Safe and sound, just like you."

"Thank you."

"My name's Jimmy. And yours is Angie—I know that. Angie's a pretty name, I think."

"Thank you," she said again, not looking at him. In fact, each of them was being so careful not to look at the other one that they were liable to trip over their own feet if they tried to walk, Fargo thought with a grin as he led the stallion over to the coach.

He handed the Ovaro's reins to Jimmy and said, "I'll go wake Mr. Grayson and Miss Grayson. We'll have to get breakfast farther on up the trail somewhere. I don't reckon we'd be welcome for a meal at the tavern, and these farmers are poor folks. I don't want to impose on their hospitality any more than we already have."

"Reckon we can get somethin' to eat at San Luis Obispo," Sandy said. "We got a few supplies left if we can't, so we won't starve to death 'fore we make Paso Robles tonight."

Fargo went to the hut where Grayson and Belinda were staying, intending to knock on the door, but it opened before he got there and Belinda stepped out, looking fresh and rested. She smiled at Fargo and said, "Good morning, Skye. Are we ready to go?"

"Just about," Fargo told her. "Is your father awake?"

"I certainly am," Grayson answered as he emerged from the hut behind Belinda. "Any trouble from that man Jarlberg this morning?"

"No, but we've picked up another passenger for the rest of the trip." Fargo waved a hand toward the coach. Angie stood beside it with Jimmy.

"Oh!" Belinda said. "That poor girl! I hoped that she might come with us, but I wasn't sure if she would want to."

"She wants to," Fargo said. "She sure doesn't want to stay here."

"Hmmph! Can't blame her for that," Grayson said. "She's more than welcome to come along. She can be the first official passenger of Grayson's California Stagecoach Line!"

With the team hitched up, the coach was ready to roll. Several of the farmers came out to say good-bye to the travelers. Fargo shook hands with them and thanked them again. The sun was just about to peek over the tops of the mountain range to the east when Fargo swung into the Ovaro's saddle and called to Sandy to move out. With a pop of the whip, a slap of the reins, and a rattle of the wheels, the coach lurched into motion and rolled along the trail, away from Los Olivos.

Fargo glanced back and thought, *Good riddance.*

*   *   *

Farther up the coast, the next stop on the original Mission Trail had been Mission La Purísima Concepción, but it had been abandoned some years earlier and was no longer a church of any sort. San Luis Obispo was still in use, and a small town was beginning to develop nearby. That was where the stage stopped at midday. The village of San Luis Obispo had an inn, and Fargo and his companions were grateful for the chance to sit down and have an actual meal there, washed down with cups of strong coffee.

When they came back out to the coach to depart, Angie surprised all of them by asking if she could ride up top on the driver's seat.

"Mighty windy up here, gal," Sandy replied with a scowl. "And if'n we was to hit a bad spot in the trail, you might get bounced right off."

"I can hang on," Angie said. Fargo had noticed during lunch that she kept stealing glances at Jimmy, and he suspected the gangling young man was the reason Angie wanted to ride on top of the stage. That way they could see each other and maybe even talk.

Jimmy said, "I think it's a good idea."

"You would," Sandy grumbled. "You just want to make calf's eyes at this poor gal."

Both of the youngsters blushed.

Belinda put a hand on Angie's shoulder and said, "I've enjoyed talking to you this morning, but if you want to ride outside, I think you should. You'll get a lot more fresh air that way."

"It's settled," Fargo said, trying not to grin at Sandy's obvious discomfiture. "Climb on up, Angie, and hang on tight."

They were still in the long valley between mountain ranges, so the afternoon's travel went fairly easily. By evening they were approaching the settlement of Paso

Robles, near the old San Miguel mission. Fargo had dropped back to ride alongside the coach on one side, while Jimmy rode on the other side, leading the spare horses.

Grayson poked his head out the window on Fargo's side, sniffed, and asked, "What's that smell? It smells like . . . brimstone."

"Don't worry," Fargo told him. "We're not coming into Hell. There are some hot springs up here at Paso Robles, and they give off that smell of sulfur."

"Hot springs, you say?" Grayson asked with sudden interest. "Such springs are very healthful. People will travel for miles to visit them. Once the stages are coming through on a regular basis, they can come to Paso Robles and bathe in the springs for their health."

Grayson was a canny businessman, always looking for some way to sell his enterprises to the public. Fargo had to give him credit for that.

In Paso Robles there was a hotel operated by a man named Houck. Out back was a stable, and that was where Sandy wheeled the stage, bringing it to a halt in a billowing cloud of dust. A couple of hundred people lived in the town, and it appeared to Fargo that most of them had heard the stagecoach coming and turned out to greet its arrival.

Kids ran around, followed by barking dogs; men stood in groups with their hands in their pockets, talking among themselves; and women held handkerchiefs over their noses to protect them from the dust. This was the biggest settlement the coach had visited since Santa Barbara, and the farthest it had deviated from the original trail between the missions.

The owner of the hotel came out to the stable to shake hands with Grayson and greet the rest of the party. "We heard you were comin'," Houck said. "It's a great day for the town o' Paso Robles. Yes, sir, a great day!"

"How did you know we were coming?" Fargo asked, surprised that word of their journey had reached the settlement ahead of them.

"Why, Mr. Stoddard told me, of course," Houck replied.

Grayson stiffened in surprise and anger. "Stoddard's here? Hiram Stoddard?"

Houck nodded. "That's right. Only he's not here anymore. He left earlier today, heading on up the coast toward Soledad."

"Damn it!" Grayson burst out. "Was he traveling by stagecoach?"

Houck looked confused as he replied, "No, him and the fellas with him were on horseback. Ain't he your partner? I got the feelin' that him and the other fellas were sort of advance men, I reckon you could say."

"No, he's not my partner. What he is, is a cutthroat son of a—"

Belinda put a hand on her father's arm, stopping him before he could finish. "Mr. Stoddard and my father are competitors," she said. "He hopes to start a stage line between Los Angeles and San Francisco, too."

Houck scratched his head. "Well, he didn't say nothin' about that. Just said you folks'd be along later."

Grayson smacked his right fist into his left hand and said, "That devil's up to something! I know it. How in the hell did he get past us?"

"Rode some at night, more than likely," Fargo said. "We wouldn't notice a few horsebackers going by on the trail."

"But I don't understand. What does he hope to accomplish by this tactic?"

Fargo could only shake his head. "I don't know . . . but I reckon if we keep going, there's a good chance we'll find out."

Fargo's main worry was that Stoddard and the men with him would set up an ambush somewhere farther along the trail. He didn't think Stoddard would stop at murder to prevent Grayson from reaching San Francisco. With Grayson dead, Stoddard could take his time about setting up his own stagecoach line along the coast.

But for tonight, anyway, they were safe, Fargo figured. Stoddard wouldn't try anything in the middle of a settlement.

Then he recalled the attempt to kidnap Belinda in Los Angeles. Maybe it would be a good idea to remain alert, just on general principles.

When Fargo discussed that with Sandy, the jehu agreed that they should continue to guard the stagecoach and the horses at night. "I'll stand the first watch," Sandy offered. "Jimmy done just fine last night, so I reckon we can trust him after all. He can take the second watch."

Fargo nodded. "And I'll finish up the night." He wondered if he would have a chance to spend some more time with Belinda tonight. Even if he did, it would probably be early enough so that it wouldn't interfere with him standing guard duty.

During dinner, Grayson and Houck had a lengthy, animated discussion about the hot springs in the area. Houck was a good businessman, too, and saw the potential in the situation right away. If he built another hotel adjacent to the springs themselves, just outside of town, Grayson's stagecoaches could make the place their regular stop in Paso Robles. Travelers could spend the night there and have a soak in the healing springs before continuing on their journey. It would be a beneficial arrangement for both men.

After dinner, Belinda drew Angie aside and said, "I think some of my dresses would fit you, dear. Why don't you come upstairs with me and we'll see about finding you something nicer to wear than that patched old dress?"

"You sure you wouldn't mind, ma'am?"

"Of course not," Belinda replied with a smile. "Come along with me."

They disappeared up the stairs to the hotel's second floor. Jimmy leaned over and said to Sandy, "I don't hardly see how Miss Angie could get any prettier than she already is."

Sandy just grumbled and scowled. "Romance!" he muttered under his breath in disgust.

Fargo smiled and left the hotel, walking out back to check on the coach and the horses. A couple of hostlers were still working in the stable, so he didn't think Stoddard would try to steal or damage the coach until later in the night, if indeed Stoddard tried anything at this point.

Sandy followed him and caught up to him as Fargo was standing at the corral fence with a booted foot propped on the bottom rail.

"Lord, that youngster's in there moonin' over that gal," Sandy complained. "He can't wait for her to come back down so he can see what she looks like dressed in some o' Miss Grayson's clothes." He spat on the ground. "O' course, you can't help but feel a mite sorry for the gal. She's had a heap o' trouble in her life. Told me about some of it this afternoon whilst she was ridin' up top with me."

"Did she say what happened to her face?" Fargo asked.

"She got a pot o' boilin' water dumped on her by

accident, some years back when she was still a kid. Lucky it just missed her left eye, or she'd've prob'ly been blinded in that one. Her folks never did treat her the same after that, even though it weren't her fault. I reckon they was worried she'd never find a husband to take her off their hands, lookin' like that."

"She looks just fine," Fargo said, "scar or no scar."

Sandy grunted. "Yeah, Jimmy sure as hell seems to think so. He's gone plumb loco over her. Asked me a while ago if I thought she'd marry up with him, if he was to ask."

"Only one way for him to find out."

"Yeah, but why'd he want to go and do a thing like that for? Hell, he might as well be puttin' his own head in the noose—"

No doubt Sandy would have gone on complaining for a while, but the sudden sound of a scream cutting through the night silenced him. He and Fargo both whirled around, well aware that the scream had come from the hotel.

And Fargo thought he recognized the voice of the woman who had let out that terrified cry.

Belinda Grayson.

10

Fargo and Sandy broke into a run toward the hotel, the Trailsman's longer legs outdistancing the shorter jehu. His Colt was already in his hand as he charged into the building and headed up the stairs, taking them two or three at a time.

Belinda hadn't screamed again, but that might not be a good thing. She might have fallen silent because something had *silenced* her.

Sandy was still huffing and puffing up the stairs when Fargo reached the second-floor landing. He grasped the banister with his free hand to help swing himself around. The corridor was crowded with folks who had heard the cry and come out of their rooms to see what was going on. They got out of the way in a hurry when they saw the grim-faced Fargo coming toward them with the big gun in his hand.

The door of Belinda's room was jerked open before Fargo got there. To his great relief, he saw Belinda and Angie in the doorway, clutching at each other, white-faced with fright as they tried to get out of the room. They stopped and Belinda exclaimed, "Skye!"

Fargo ran his gaze over both young women. As far as he could see, they were unharmed. Angie was wearing one of Belinda's gowns and looked very nice in it, despite being scared.

"Are you two all right?" Fargo asked as he came up to them.

Belinda nodded and said, "Yes, just . . . just frightened. We saw . . ." She swallowed, unable to go on for a moment.

"It was awful," Angie put in. "Just awful."

"What?" Fargo prodded.

Belinda said, *"A ghost."*

Fargo's eyes narrowed. He might have expected her to say a lot of things, but that wasn't one of them.

"A ghost?" he repeated.

Belinda and Angie both nodded. "It was outside the window of my room, hanging in midair and . . . and glowing."

"It was a man's face," Angie added. "The spookiest thing I ever saw."

She had become more talkative as the day went on, as familiarity with her new companions overcame her ingrained shyness, and now the words bubbled out of her.

"His face was lit up and he gave out this terrible moan and I never saw anything like it in all my borned days! Me and Miss Grayson were so scared we grabbed on to each other, and she let out a yell, and then we stood there too scared to move for a minute."

"What happened to the ghost?" Fargo asked.

Belinda and Angie looked at each other. "I—I don't know," Belinda admitted. "It must have disappeared when I screamed."

Angie shook her head. "I was so shook up I never noticed when it vanished."

Sandy had come up behind Fargo, along with Jimmy, Grayson, and Houck, who had still been downstairs talking when Belinda screamed. The hotel owner declared, "There are no ghosts in this place. I just built it last year, and nobody's died here. I'd appreciate it if you folks wouldn't go around sayin' that it's haunted, because that'll be mighty bad for my business."

Fargo didn't really care about Houck's business. He just wanted to get to the bottom of this incident.

"You said this so-called ghost was a man. What did he look like?"

"Well . . ." Belinda hesitated. "He wasn't young. He had a bald head."

Like a padre with a tonsure, Fargo thought.

"And he looked really sad," Angie said. "Like something terrible had happened."

They were describing Father Tomás, the padre from San Buenaventura that the old hostler had told Fargo about a couple of mornings earlier. Fargo might have believed that the young women had been seeing things because of that ghost story . . . if not for the fact that he hadn't told Belinda about it, and Angie hadn't even been with them at the time.

"Let me take a look," Fargo said as he stepped into the room. He started toward the window. The curtains were pushed back.

"Be careful, Skye," Belinda said.

He looked back at her. "Were these curtains open when you first saw whatever it was?"

"It was a ghost," Angie muttered.

Belinda said, "No, they were closed, but they're thin enough so that I noticed the glow through them. I went over and pushed them back like they are now."

Fargo nodded. The window was closed. With his free hand, he grasped it and raised it. He stuck his head out for a moment, then pulled it back in.

"Well, there's your answer," he said.

Belinda took a couple of tentative steps closer to the window. "What?"

"There's a balcony out there."

"Yeah, there is," Houck put in.

"Somebody had to be standing on it and peeking in the window," Fargo said.

Belinda thought about that, frowned, and shook her head. "That doesn't explain why he was glowing, or how he disappeared like that."

"All he had to do to disappear was duck down and walk away," Fargo pointed out. "He could have climbed over the railing around the balcony and dropped to the street without any trouble."

"What about the way he looked?"

Fargo didn't have an answer for that one.

Grayson asked, "Did this man threaten you in any way, Belinda? I'm thinking that he could have been someone who's working for Stoddard."

"No, he didn't do anything except stand there and look . . . mournful, like he had lost his best friend."

"Sounds like a haint to me," Sandy said, ignoring the glare that Houck sent in his direction. The hotel man turned and started shooing people back to their rooms, telling them that there was nothing to see, nothing to worry about.

"Whatever happened, it seems to be over," Fargo said. "I reckon we can all get back to what we were doing."

"I'm not sleeping in here by myself tonight," Belinda declared. "Not after that."

"I could stay with you, miss," Angie offered. "I'd be glad to help out, after all you folks have done for me."

Belinda smiled and hugged the younger girl. "Thank you, Angie. I'll take you up on that, if you're sure you don't mind."

"No, ma'am."

There went any chance of him and Belinda getting together again tonight, Fargo thought. But after being spooked like that, she probably wouldn't have been in much of a mood for lovemaking, anyway.

Besides, he planned to do a little prowling around himself tonight.

Ghost hunting, he reckoned it could be called.

Fargo didn't tell anyone except Sandy about Father Tomás and the story he had heard from the hostler at San Buenaventura. He waited until they were alone in the stable, making a last check on the horses, before he brought it up.

When Fargo was finished, Sandy scratched his beard and said, "Yeah, now that I think about it, I've heard o' that old yarn, too. But it's just a legend. Ain't really nothin' to it."

"I imagine the part about the stolen treasure is true," Fargo said.

"Yeah, but I don't reckon I believe in haints and spirits and such-like. Anyway, even if the ghost o' that old padre is still wanderin' around San Buenaventura, what would he be doin' all the way up here sneakin' a peek at them gals?"

"I don't know, but I'd hazard a guess that it's connected with Stoddard somehow."

"You gonna tell anybody else about this here Father Tomás?"

Fargo shook his head. "Not just yet. The ladies would just be more convinced than ever that they saw a real ghost."

"Maybe they did," Sandy muttered. "I ain't sayin' I believe in such things, mind you, but ever' so often you run across somethin' that just can't be explained."

" 'There are more things in heaven and earth, Horatio, than are dreamt of in your philosophy'," Fargo quoted.

"Huh? Who's this Horatio fella?"

Fargo shook his head. "Never mind. You're still taking the first watch?"

"Yeah." Sandy hefted the double-barreled shotgun he carried. "If any haints come around botherin' me, I'll give 'em a buckshot welcome."

"That goes for Stoddard and his men, too, I hope."

"Damn tootin'."

Fargo walked back to the hotel, leaving Sandy in the stable. To his surprise, when he went in the back door of the building he found Belinda Grayson waiting for him.

"I have to talk to you, Skye."

He glanced toward the second floor. "You left Angie up there by herself?"

"The poor dear was worn-out. She went right to sleep, even after that scare we had." Belinda's forehead creased in a solemn frown. "That's what I want to talk to you about. We saw something odd at San Buenaventura, remember? I want to know if there's a connection between what we saw at the mission there and what happened tonight."

Fargo could tell from the stubborn look on her face that she wasn't going to accept any evasive answers he might give her. Since there was no point in even trying to deceive her, he nodded and said, "Maybe. The old man at that stable told me a story. . . ."

Belinda waited. Fargo launched into the story of Father Tomás and the pirate Bouchard and the stolen treasure. As he talked, Belinda's expression became one of amazement.

"That's it!" she said when he was finished. "That has to be the answer. The man Angie and I saw looked like he could have been a priest. I mean, we didn't see anything but his face, so I don't know if he was wearing a priest's robe, but he had that sort of mournful air about him. He had to be the ghost of Father Tomás!"

"Just one thing wrong with that," Fargo said.

"What?"

"You have to believe in ghosts to accept that idea."

"Oh." She frowned again. "Well, yes, that's true, I suppose. But do you have a more reasonable explanation, Skye?"

"You saw one of Stoddard's men spying on you."

"Why would anyone do that?" She blushed a little. "Other than the most obvious reason, I mean."

Fargo had been thinking about it, and now he said, "Maybe he wanted to be sure which room you were staying in, so that they can try to kidnap you again."

Belinda's eyes widened. "Do you think that's possible?"

"From what I've seen so far of Stoddard and the varmints who work for him, I wouldn't put much of anything past them."

"Neither would I. Oh, dear Lord! I left Angie up there all alone. They might grab her thinking that she's me!"

That was a legitimate worry, Fargo thought. He took hold of Belinda's arm and said, "Let's go make sure she's still all right."

To their relief, Angie was sleeping soundly when Belinda eased the door of the room open a few moments later, and the two of them looked in on her.

"I'll find Houck and see what we can do about switching you ladies to another room," Fargo said. "Wait here, but don't doze off."

"Not much chance of that," Belinda said. "Not after everything that's happened tonight."

"Yell if anything odd happens."

"You can count on it, Skye."

Belinda went in to wake up Angie and tell her they were going to change rooms while Fargo went in search of the hotel owner. He found Houck downstairs, still talking business with Arthur Grayson. When Fargo explained the situation, both men thought it would be a good idea to put Belinda and Angie in a different room.

It didn't take long to accomplish that. When it was done, everyone settled down for the night except Fargo, who stepped outside again briefly. A wind was blowing in from the sea, scudding clouds across the moon. It was a wild sky, Fargo thought as he looked up at it, the sort of sky you would see on a night when anything could happen.

He halfway expected to see the spectral figure of a long-dead padre floating through the darkness.

But there was nothing unusual stirring around the hotel, and after a few minutes he went back inside. No ghosts haunted his sleep that night.

The next morning at breakfast, Belinda and Angie reported no more ghostly visitations. It had been quiet in the stable, too, as no one attempted to bother the coach or the horses.

In a way, that lack of activity on Stoddard's part concerned Fargo. Two more days of travel would see the coach arriving in San Francisco. Fargo was sure that Stoddard would strike before they arrived in the city by the bay, and when the blow finally came, it was liable to be a particularly vicious one.

Angie looked good in another of Belinda's dresses, and Fargo was surprised to see that her long blond hair had been brushed until it shone and then pulled back behind her head in a flattering arrangement. That made her scarred cheek more visible, but she was so slender and graceful that no one paid much attention to that imperfection. Jimmy certainly didn't. He was staring at her with such open admiration that it seemed to be all he could do to keep his eyes in his head.

The coach was rolling again not long after sunup, with Houck standing in front of the hotel waving farewell to the pilgrims.

As they continued northward, the valley began to narrow as the mountains closed in from both sides. The terrain was marshy in places, and Fargo didn't care for it. He liked higher ground and more wide-open spaces. The air here was sticky and abuzz with insects. The Ovaro flicked his ears and swatted his tail in annoyance as the bugs swarmed around him.

The travelers stopped for their midday meal in the town of Salinas, then pressed on. Fargo had planned for them to spend the night in Soledad, but they were making such good time that they might reach San Juan Bautista, he decided. Remembering the maps he had studied in Grayson's hotel room in Los Angeles and his previous trips through this area, he knew that soon they would be coming to a fork in the Old Mission Trail. One way, to the right, led to San Juan Bautista. To the left was San Carlos Borroméo de Carmelo, right on the coast with the town of Monterey nearby. The terrain was much more rugged in that direction, so he intended to bear right and go through San Juan Bautista.

Once the marshes were behind them and they had passed the turnoff for Monterey, the valley grew even more narrow and trees began to close in on either side of the trail. Riding about two hundred yards ahead of the coach, Fargo felt the skin on the back of his neck prickle as some instinct kicked in to warn him. They were headed straight into what might be a prime spot for an ambush.

No sooner had the thought crossed his mind than a rifle cracked somewhere up ahead and he heard the wind rip of a bullet pass his ear. Fargo hauled back on the reins and whirled the Ovaro around, then sent the stallion racing back toward the stagecoach. Another slug whined over his head.

Sandy had already heard the shots and was sawing on the reins as he brought the coach to a halt. "Get inside and keep your head down!" he snapped at Angie. Looking back at Jimmy, he shouted, "Turn them horses around!"

Fargo saw Angie leap down from the driver's seat and climb in through the door of the coach, which Belinda had opened for her. The older girl closed the door and looked out at Fargo as he galloped up. Her face was pale with fear.

"All of you stay down!" he called to the passengers. "Sandy, there's no place for us to go but back the way we came from!"

"Damned if I don't know it!" the jehu said. "This blasted trail's almost too narrow to turn around in!"

"I'll keep them off your back while you're doing it," Fargo said. He pulled the Sharps from the saddle sheath strapped to the Ovaro and swung around toward the bushwhackers. By now, several men on horseback had emerged from their hiding places among the trees on either side of the road and were galloping toward the coach, firing handguns as they came.

Fargo lifted the heavy carbine to his shoulder and called, "Take the Monterey road!" to Sandy. He eased back the hammer on the Sharps, drew a bead on one of the attackers, and pressed the trigger.

The Ovaro, calm and steady under fire as always, stood motionless and gave him a good platform from which to aim.

The Sharps roared and kicked hard against Fargo's shoulder. As the smoke from the barrel blew across in front of Fargo's face, he saw one of the bushwhackers fly out of the saddle, arms and legs pinwheeling as the heavy slug drove him backward.

The range was still a little great for revolvers. Fargo sat there coolly and reloaded the Sharps. When he lifted it again, the charging gunmen tried to rein in and peel off to the sides, realizing that one of them was about to gallop right into a faceful of death.

They didn't react fast enough. Fargo fired again, and a second man jerked as the Trailsman's lead ripped into him. The wounded man managed to stay in the saddle, but he sagged forward over his horse's neck, obviously out of the fight.

Fargo glanced over his shoulder. With the skill that years of experience handling the reins had given him, Sandy had backed and turned the stagecoach until it was pointed toward the other direction. He shouted at the horses and popped the whip as he slashed at their rumps with the reins. The team lunged against its harness and sent the stage careening back down the trail.

Fargo wheeled the stallion around and was about to gallop after the stagecoach when a giant fist came out of nowhere, smashed into the side of his head, and sent him plummeting into darkness. He didn't feel the ground come up and smash into him, because he was already out cold when he fell.

11

Fargo regained consciousness less than a minute later, although he didn't know at the moment that such a short period of time had passed. He heard shooting and shouting. Hoofbeats hammered on the ground somewhere close by. He forced himself to roll onto his hands and knees, and groped for his Colt as he struggled to stand up.

A strong hand gripped his arm and helped him to his feet. "You all right, Mr. Fargo?" Jimmy asked. "I hope so, 'cause here they come again!"

Fargo looked up and saw that the gunmen were once again charging toward them, just as Jimmy had said.

"It's gonna be a real battle," the young man went on. "Just like when Joaquin and Three-Fingered Jack shot it out with the rangers!"

"I'd just as soon not wind up with my head in a jar," Fargo said as he lifted his Colt. "Let 'em have it!"

Standing shoulder to shoulder in the road, he and Jimmy opened fire as bullets kicked up dust around their feet. Jimmy had to be scared, but he didn't show it. He seemed cool and collected as he squeezed off shot after shot from his old pistol. Fargo took his time, too, aiming before he pulled the trigger each time.

Clouds of powder smoke rolled over them, stinging their noses and half blinding them.

But Fargo was able to hear the angry yell from one of the bushwhackers. "Damn it, let's get out of here! The bastards are shootin' us to ribbons!"

"Split up!" Fargo told Jimmy. "Head for the trees and reload, in case they come back!"

With his head pounding, he picked up his hat, ran into the shelter of the trees to his right, and began reloading the Colt, which he had emptied at the attackers. He had to pause to wipe blood out of his right eye, where it had dripped from the cut on the side of his head while he was unconscious. The bullet that had struck him barely grazed him, a mere kiss, but that had been enough to knock him out of the saddle and make him lose consciousness for a moment. Fargo was confident that it hadn't done any permanent damage, though.

He closed the Colt's cylinder and peered along the trail. The bushwhackers had fled. He saw no sign of them. But that didn't mean they weren't lurking somewhere close by, waiting for another chance to try to kill him and his companions.

"Mr. Fargo, are you all right?" Jimmy called from the other side of the trail. "I know you were hit by one of those shots."

"Just a scratch, Jimmy," Fargo assured him. "I may have a headache tomorrow, but it takes more than that to dent this thick skull of mine." Fargo looked the other way along the trail. The stagecoach and the spare horses were out of sight, too. "You shouldn't have come back to help me. I was counting on you to stay with the coach."

"Shoot, when I saw you fall, I couldn't just leave you. And them fellas might've trampled you if I hadn't come back."

Fargo gave a grim chuckle. "They might have, at that. I'm much obliged to you, Jimmy."

"My pleasure. Now I can say I fought side by side with the famous Trailsman."

Fargo wasn't sure just how great an honor that really was, but he let it pass. He said, "You didn't just let the spare horses go, did you?"

"Nope, I managed to throw the lead rope to Angie, and she hung out the window and tied it to the rail on top of the coach. She's a mighty brave girl, as well as bein' mighty pretty."

Fargo couldn't argue with either of those things. "Where's your saddle horse?"

"He ran off into the woods. I reckon he was scared, what with all the shootin' goin' on. Your stallion went with him."

Fargo nodded, not surprised by what the young man had just told him. He whistled, and a moment later the Ovaro emerged from the trees, driving the other horse in front of him with an occasional nip at the animal's rump. Fargo figured that the stallion had gotten out of the line of fire. Now that the shooting was over, the Ovaro came back and brought Jimmy's horse with him.

The men stepped out into the trail, grabbed the reins, and swung up into their saddles. "Let's go see if we can find that stagecoach," Fargo said.

Sandy had done like Fargo told him and taken the trail that led to the settlement of Monterey and San Carlos Borroméo, sometimes known as Mission Carmel. The trail twisted through the pine-covered mountains that ran almost all the way to the ocean before dropping off in a series of spectacular cliffs. The rugged terrain slowed the stagecoach enough so that

Fargo and Jimmy were able to catch up to it before it reached the seaside settlement of Monterey.

"Jimmy!" Angie called from the window of the coach as she looked back along the trail and saw them coming. She stuck an arm out and gave them an enthusiastic wave that Jimmy returned with equal enthusiasm.

Sandy slowed the coach to a stop and let Fargo and Jimmy ride up alongside it. Belinda saw the dried blood on the side of Fargo's face and exclaimed, "Skye, you're hurt!"

"Just a scratch," the Trailsman assured her, "nothing to worry about."

"Those were Stoddard's men who ambushed us, weren't they?" Grayson said.

Fargo nodded. "I'm pretty sure I saw that hombre Elam, who was working for Stoddard down in Los Angeles. The others were probably gunmen he picked up on the way up here. There are plenty of men in California who are handy with a Colt and willing to use it for the right price."

"What are we going to do now? We can't go back the way we had planned, can we?"

"No, they'll be laying for us that way," Fargo said with a shake of his head. "But that's not the only trail to San Francisco. We'll go on to Monterey and stick close to the coast."

Grayson's forehead furrowed in a worried frown. "That's going to be an awfully rough trail. It's not the way I'd normally take a stagecoach."

"It's not the way I'd go, either," Fargo agreed, "but Stoddard's bushwhackers sort of changed the rules of this game. I know we were supposed to follow the best route, but now it's a matter of just getting to San Francisco alive, so you can prove that a stagecoach can make it through. Once you've done that, you can change the route later if you want to."

Grayson nodded in acceptance of Fargo's reasoning. "You're right, of course. The important thing is making it through alive. So it's on to Monterey?"

"On to Monterey," Fargo said.

They reached the settlement just as the sun was dipping below the surface of the ocean to the west, painting the clouds and the sky in an awe-inspiring display of colors. The picturesque houses of Monterey, with their mixture of Spanish and American architecture, the darkly looming, pine-covered hills, the vast ocean and the endlessly crashing waves . . . it all combined to make as pretty a scene as Fargo had witnessed in quite some time.

They stopped at a hotel with a red-tiled roof, built around a central plaza with a fountain. Fargo reckoned the place had been there ever since Spanish explorers had settled the area many years earlier.

The stagecoach's arrival was unexpected, but the travelers received a hearty welcome anyway. The hotel owner wanted to know if the coach would be making a regular run through Monterey in the future. Grayson hedged on answering that. The main line wouldn't run through here, Fargo thought . . . but Grayson might want to consider setting up a feeder line to give people more access to the coast.

While the others were tending to the horses and getting settled in the hotel, Fargo went in search of a doctor. He was pretty sure his head was all right, but it wouldn't hurt anything to have a medico take a look at the wound.

The sawbones he found was an elderly Mexican named Zapata. The man fussed at Fargo as he cleaned the wound. "You should not go around getting shot at," Zapata complained. "Young men are too reckless."

"It wasn't my idea to have to duck some flying lead," Fargo told him. "Anyway," he added with a smile, "I'll bet in your day you did a few reckless things."

Zapata gave a dignified sniff and said, "I prefer not to think about such things." Memory overtook him, though, and he grinned. "Perhaps you are right, senor."

Once the dried blood had been cleaned away and Zapata had examined the wound, he announced that it would not require stitches.

"I will bandage the wound to keep it clean, but other than that, everything should be fine." The old man leaned closer to Fargo. "Let me see your eyes."

Fargo met the doctor's gaze. Zapata studied his eyes for a few moments and then gave a satisfied grunt.

"They look fine. No injury to your brain, in my opinion. You are a lucky man, Senor Fargo. An inch or two to the side, as they say . . ." The doctor's shoulders rose and fell in an expressive shrug.

"Yeah, but an inch or two the other way and it would have missed me," Fargo pointed out with a smile.

"One could look at it like that," Zapata admitted as he finished wrapping a bandage around Fargo's head so that the bullet crease was covered. "The bill for my services will be one dollar, American."

Fargo paid Zapata and then put his hat on, being careful how he did it. The hat covered the bandage for the most part and didn't hurt his head too much. Fargo left the doctor's office and headed back to the hotel.

It was a gracious place, and despite his slight headache, he enjoyed the supper that the group had in the dining room. As they ate, Arthur Grayson asked, "Will we still make San Francisco tomorrow?"

"Hard to say," Fargo replied. "If we follow the coastline around Monterey Bay, we can hit the Old Mission Trail again at Santa Cruz. From there it'll be a pretty straight shot on up the peninsula to San Francisco. Whether or not we make it tomorrow depends on how rough the trail is between here and Santa Cruz . . . and whether we run into any more trouble along the way."

"Oh, we'll run into trouble," Grayson said. "Hiram Stoddard's not going to give up at this point. He'll do whatever it takes to stop me from beating him."

Fargo thought that was pretty likely, too.

Jimmy and Angie were still making eyes at each other. Angie thought it was very brave of Jimmy to have gone back to help Fargo like that. Fargo pointed out that Jimmy might well have saved his life. The young man blushed and muttered and acted embarrassed, but it was clear that he enjoyed the attention.

Maybe when the time came for Jimmy to return to Los Angeles, Angie would go with him, Fargo thought. That might just be the best solution all the way around.

The night watch was split into four shifts, with Fargo, Grayson, Sandy, and Jimmy each taking a turn. Fargo had the first watch tonight, so he took his Sharps and walked down the street to the wagon yard where the stagecoach had been parked. The teams were in the stable next door.

Nothing happened during Fargo's shift. Grayson showed up on schedule, and Fargo told him that all was quiet.

"It won't stay that way," Grayson said with a pessimistic scowl. He took a cigar from his vest pocket and clamped it between his teeth, leaving it there unlit.

Fargo returned to the hotel. When he reached his room upstairs, he was surprised to find one of the servants there pouring hot water from a bucket into a large tub that was already mostly full.

"I didn't order a bath," Fargo said with a frown.

The servant, a stout Mexican woman, just shrugged and said, "I was told to prepare it, senor. Perhaps it was a mistake and was supposed to be in some other room. But the tub is here and full of hot water. Perhaps you should enjoy the blessings of good fortune."

Fargo couldn't argue with that. He gave the woman a coin and sent her on her way, then started stripping off his dusty buckskins.

When he was naked, he stepped into the tub, wincing a little at the feel of the hot water. He grimaced even more as he lowered himself into it. His body was still sore and covered with bruises from the fracas with Jarlberg back at Los Olivos. Those bruises all twinged as the hot water hit them.

But then, as the heat washed through Fargo, the aches and pains began to ease. He leaned his head back and closed his eyes. A delicious feeling of languor enveloped him. After a few minutes like that, he didn't hurt at all, not even his wounded head.

Fargo knew that some people considered regular baths to be unhealthful. At the same time, hot springs like the ones down at Paso Robles were always popular. This tub wasn't full of minerals like hot springs were, but the heat soothed away Fargo's worries anyway.

Under the circumstances, he could have been forgiven if he hadn't noticed the door of his room opening. But he did notice, and his eyes were open and the Colt he had placed on a chair beside the tub was ready in his hand by the time the door swung open.

"Skye, I thought you'd be glad to see me," Belinda said with a pout.

"Oh, I am," Fargo told her as he smiled and placed the gun back on the chair. Understanding dawned on him. "You're the one who ordered this tub for me, aren't you?"

She wore the thin silk robe that clung to her enticing curves. Fargo hadn't been able to tell what color it was before, because of the darkness in the farmer's hut. Now, in the light of the lamp that was trimmed low on the bedside table, he saw that the garment was a deep forest green. It looked beautiful on her, and she definitely looked beautiful in it.

But she looked even more beautiful when she untied the belt, shrugged out of the robe, let it fall around her feet, and stood nude before him.

"Is there room in there for me?" she murmured.

"I don't know," Fargo told her. "Why don't you find out?"

She came over to him and stepped daintily into the tub. "It's hot," she said as her foot touched the water.

From where he was sitting, looking up at her with one leg raised to step into the tub, he could only agree with her. Hot, indeed.

She eased down into the water, saying, "Ooohhh," as she sank into the heat. It was pretty cramped in the tub with both of them in it, but neither of them minded being pressed together. Belinda moved her legs so that they were around Fargo's hips. She sat on his thighs. His manhood jutted up between them, stiff as a bar of iron.

Belinda's position put her breasts right in front of Fargo's face. He leaned forward to run his tongue around the hard nipple that crowned her right breast. She closed her eyes in pleasure as he licked at the pebbled bud of flesh. Fargo sucked on the right nipple for a moment, then moved over to the left one.

While he was doing that, she reached down into the

hot water and closed both hands around his shaft. Slow strokes, her soft palms gliding over him, increased his arousal that much more. In turn, he sucked a little harder on the left breast while he cupped and squeezed the right one.

"Oh, Skye," Belinda whispered.

For long moments they stayed there like that, taking their time as they luxuriated in the caresses they bestowed on each other. Delicious sensations spilled through Fargo, surging through his veins and along his nerves, sensations hot as fire, cold as ice, thrilling in their promise, tantalizing in their delay. With the dangers that had faced them all the way in this journey, they never knew when each encounter might be their last, so Fargo wanted to make the most of this. He wanted it to be something that neither of them would ever forget.

At last he slipped his hands below the water, cupped her buttocks, and lifted her, bringing her closer to him. When he lowered her, the head of his member found her drenched opening with unerring aim. She slid down onto him, taking him deep inside her.

Belinda wrapped her arms around Fargo's neck and kissed him. The slow writhing of her hips excited both of them and felt exquisite. Fargo suppressed the urge to drive into her fast and hard. This was a time for being deliberate. He embraced her so that her breasts flattened against his chest. She thrust her tongue into his mouth, invading his body as he was plundering hers.

The two of them were so close, joined so intimately, that they seemed more like one being than two. Fargo's hips flexed, making him move deep inside her. A slow shudder that seemed to reach all the way to her core rolled through her, and as Fargo felt it he surrendered to his own culmination, which had been growing in urgency until he was ready to explode. Buried within her, holding her as tightly as he could, he allowed his climax to gush out, filling her.

Drained, he slumped against the sloping back of the tub. He let himself slide down until his head was under the water and took Belinda with him. When they came up a second later, they were both soaked and laughing. Belinda shook her head to get the wet hair out of her eyes.

"I thought there would be room for me, too," she said. "I'm glad there was."

"So am I," Fargo agreed. He was still hard, still buried to the hilt in her.

She couldn't help but notice that. "Skye," she said in amazement, "you can't be ready to go again so soon!"

"No, but if you want to just sit here for a while and give me a chance to catch my breath, who knows? Maybe the water won't get too cold while we're waiting."

She laughed again. "I don't care if it does!"

Fargo cradled her in his arms as she rested her head on his shoulder. It felt so good holding her like that; he might have been happy just to stay that way for the rest of the night, no matter how much the water cooled off. It didn't even matter that much whether they made love again or not.

There was no telling what might have happened if they had been undisturbed.

Unfortunately, as had happened before during this journey, the pleasant interlude was interrupted.

Interrupted by a cry in the night, a frightened scream.

Here we go again, Fargo thought.

12

He stood up, still holding on to Belinda, and set her out of the tub onto the floor as she gasped.

"Skye, that sounded like Angie!"

"I know," Fargo said as he reached for his trousers. He pulled them on as fast as he could, grabbed his Colt, and headed for the door in his bare feet. "Stay here!" he flung over his shoulder at Belinda.

He raced out into the corridor and turned toward Angie's room. Another scream came from her as he reached her door. He grabbed the knob and twisted, and the door came open. Fargo was grateful for that. If the heavy panel had been locked, it would have taken him a while to break it down.

As Fargo lunged into the room, the light that spilled in with him from the hall showed Angie sitting up in bed, the covers pulled around her throat, eyes wide with fright and turned toward the window. She looked at Fargo and screamed again before she realized who he was. Then she cried, "Mr. Fargo! The window! The window!"

Fargo had already figured out that was the most likely source of danger. He leaped toward the window. The night breeze billowed the curtains. Flame geysered from the muzzle of a gun, like an orange flower in the darkness.

Fargo darted aside as the bullet whipped past his head. The muzzle flash had half blinded him, but not before he'd caught a glimpse of a face at the window. *Father Tomás?* he asked himself as he brought his Colt up.

Not hardly. Ghosts didn't use hoglegs.

Fargo snapped a shot at the window, but the face had already dropped out of sight. Fargo put his back against the wall next to the window, knowing that if he stuck his head out, he would be offering it as a prime target.

But he couldn't just stay there and let whoever had been lurking outside get away again. He snapped at Angie, "Roll off the other side of the bed, get down on the floor, and stay there!"

Then, as he heard running footsteps hammering the hard-packed dirt of the road outside, he dropped to a crouch and risked a look out the window.

A wrought-iron trellis reached up the wall nearly to the window. That was how the hombre had gotten there. Now he was running away as fast as he could through the darkness. Fargo caught a glimpse of the fleeing figure and fired without taking the time to aim.

The Trailsman's instincts were good. The running man stumbled, fell, and rolled over before trying to struggle back to his feet. Fargo's shot had hit him, but not hard enough to put him down and keep him down.

Fargo swung a leg over the windowsill and climbed out, using his feet, his free hand, and his natural agility to scramble halfway down the trellis. That put him low enough to let go and drop the rest of the way to the street.

As his feet hit the ground, he saw the man who had taken the shot at him running away again. Fargo wanted answers more than he wanted revenge for the attempt on his life, so he sprinted after the fleeing figure instead of squeezing off another shot or two.

The man was stumbling, obviously hurt. He twisted around as he ran. Fargo veered to the left as the man fired. The bullet screamed off into the night. Fargo held his fire, even though he had closed the gap now to a point where he could have downed the lurker with another shot.

Weaving to the right, Fargo avoided another slug. He heard his quarry panting with the effort of running. As Fargo drew closer, he gathered his muscles and then launched himself forward in a diving tackle.

He slammed into the back of the man's legs, his arms wrapping around them and pulling him down. The man let out a muffled curse as he fell.

They landed heavily in the street. Fargo was up first, leaping to his feet and lashing out with a foot as the man tried to twist around and bring a gun to bear. Fargo's foot connected with the man's wrist and sent the revolver spinning off into the darkness. Fargo dropped to his knees, driving one of them into the man's midsection. He jammed the barrel of the Colt under the man's chin.

"Settle down or I'll blow your damn head off," Fargo grated. He wanted the man alive, but the hombre didn't have to know that.

The man stopped struggling and just lay there gasping in breathlessness and pain. After a moment, he groaned. "I'm shot," he said. "Damn it, I'm shot."

"You're lucky you're not dead," Fargo told him. Keeping the gun trained on his prisoner, he stood up and took a step back. "Get up."

"I'm hurt, I tell you! You put a bullet in my side, mister."

"If you don't want one in your head, you'll get on your feet."

With a lot of cursing and complaining, the lurker managed to climb upright. Fargo marched him back toward the hotel. The man kept his right arm clamped to his side where Fargo's bullet had torn through him.

Several men emerged from the hotel before Fargo and his prisoner got there, including Sandy and Jimmy, both of whom were armed and looking for somebody to shoot. One of the other men held a lantern, raising it over his head so that its light washed over the street.

"Fargo!" Sandy said. "Miss Angie said you took off after a bushwhacker. I figured you'd bring him back."

From the porch of the hotel, Belinda called, "That's no bushwhacker! That's our ghost!" She and Angie had come out of the hotel wrapped in thick robes, not like the thin, clinging one Belinda had been wearing earlier.

"Ghost, hell!" Sandy said. "Don't look like no padre to me."

"What padre?" Angie asked. She hadn't heard the story of Father Tomás yet.

Fargo didn't want to confuse the issue with ghost stories. He said to one of the bystanders, "How about fetching the local law and the doctor? This fella's wounded."

The man was reluctant to leave, probably afraid he would miss something exciting, but after a second he nodded and hurried off down the street.

Several wicker chairs were lined up on the hotel porch. Fargo sat the prisoner down in one of them and stood in front of him, gun in hand. "Who the hell are you, mister?" he demanded. "And why have you been sneaking around and spying on these ladies?"

"I need a sawbones," the man groaned: "I'm in terrible pain."

Fargo eared back the hammer of the Colt. "You'll hurt worse if you don't answer my questions."

"All right, all right! Damn it. . . . My name's Harry Keller."

He was a medium-sized man in his thirties, but despite his relatively young age his head was mostly bald, with only a fringe of hair around his ears. He wore a cowhide vest over a homespun shirt and corduroy trousers. His empty holster was attached to a gun belt strapped around his waist.

"You work for Hiram Stoddard, don't you, Keller?" Fargo asked.

Keller looked surprised. "Yeah. But he ain't payin' me enough to keep quiet when some loco bastard's threatenin' me with a gun!"

Fargo let that "loco bastard" comment pass. He asked again, "Why have you been spying on the young ladies?"

"Stoddard told me to keep an eye on them and spook 'em if I could. He wanted them to think a ghost was after 'em so maybe the Grayson girl would get scared and try to talk her father into turnin' back. That's why—that's why I got a little candle and held it inside a glass under my face, so the light would shine up on it and make me look scary."

"It worked," Belinda said. "At least the scary part." She gave a defiant toss of her head. "But if Stoddard thought that would make me try to get my father to give up, he was dead wrong!"

Fargo asked, "How did Stoddard find out about Father Tomás?"

"Who's Father Tomás?" Angie said. "What's going on here?"

Keller said, "We talked to that old hostler down at San Buenaventura. We knew you'd spent the night there. The Mex didn't want to tell us anything at first, but Stoddard had Elam rough him up."

Fargo's jaw clenched in anger. He hoped the old-timer wasn't hurt too bad. That was just one more score to settle with Stoddard.

"He told us you'd seen their local ghost there at the mission and that he'd explained the whole story to you, Fargo," Keller went on. "Stoddard figured you told Miss Grayson about it. He wanted to come up with some way to slow you down or maybe get you to turn back, so he decided to try this ghost business." The hired gunman grimaced as a fresh wave of pain came from the bullet wound in his side. "I wish he'd picked somebody else to play the damn ghost, though!"

"You're lucky I just winged you," Fargo snapped. "Are you sure all you were doing was trying to scare them?"

"Yeah," Keller insisted, but after a moment under Fargo's steady glare, he shrugged. "Stoddard wanted me to keep track of which room Miss Grayson was in, too, just in case he decided to try to grab her."

Fargo nodded. "I thought so."

As several men hurried up, Fargo recognized Dr. Zapata among them. One of the other newcomers was a stocky gent with a scattergun in his hands and a lawman's badge pinned to his coat. "What's all this commotion about?" the star packer demanded. "Folks runnin' around shootin' off guns in the middle o' the night! It ain't decent!"

"Neither is what this hombre was doing," Fargo said as he gestured toward Keller. While Zapata was patching up the hole in the gunman's side as best he could under these conditions, Fargo explained to the sheriff what had happened.

When Fargo was finished, the lawman turned to Zapata and asked, "Is this fella in good enough shape I can lock him up, Doc?"

"He will be if I can take him over to my office for a while first," Zapata replied. "This wound needs to be cleaned and bandaged better than I can do the job here."

"All right." The sheriff gestured with the twin barrels of his shotgun. "On your feet, mister, and march over to the doc's office. Then you're goin' to jail."

Keller cast a baleful glance at Fargo and muttered a curse before he walked off with the sheriff, Zapata, and several of the citizens of Monterey who were going along to make sure that the gunman didn't try to cause any more trouble.

"Well, I reckon that answers one question," Sandy said. "There ain't no ghost trailin' us."

"No," Fargo said, "just another of Stoddard's troublemakers."

"And we ain't seen the last o' them, have we?"

Fargo shook his head. "I'm afraid not."

Arthur Grayson had heard the shooting but had been reluctant to leave his post guarding the stagecoach and the horses, for fear that someone was trying to lure him away so the horses could be stolen or the stagecoach damaged. That meant he didn't know what had happened until Sandy relieved him and explained about the "ghost."

"Is there anything at all Stoddard won't stoop to in order to get what he wants?" Grayson asked at breakfast the next morning.

"I reckon we'll find out today," Fargo said.

A grim silence greeted his comment. They all knew what he meant. Since it was possible they would reach San Francisco by the end of the day, this would be Stoddard's last chance to stop them.

A narrow trail ran along the top of the cliffs around Monterey Bay, Fargo recalled from previous visits to the area. A man on horseback could negotiate the path without too much trouble, but a stagecoach was a different matter. Sandy would have to use great care in handling the reins, especially on some of the hairpin turns.

As the coach pulled out after breakfast, Fargo couldn't shake the feeling that they had been herded into taking this route. Maybe the ambush on the road to San Juan Bautista hadn't been meant to stop them. Maybe Stoddard's goal had been to force them onto this trail instead, where he would have an even easier time getting rid of them.

Fargo didn't know what Stoddard's plans were, but he rode with the Sharps across the saddle in front of him, ready for trouble.

If anything, the scenery was even more spectacular here than farther south. To Fargo's left, the cliffs plunged a couple of hundred feet to jagged rocks where the waves crashed and foamed. To his right rose a steep, rocky slope dotted with pine trees. A brisk updraft blew from the sea, bringing with it the smell of brine. God had done some mighty fine work here along the coast of California. Fargo would have enjoyed riding through these parts, if he hadn't known that it was only a matter of time before Stoddard struck again. He was afraid that today, with Stoddard still on the loose, God's back might be turned.

They were halfway around the bay when a low rumbling sound made Fargo stiffen in the saddle. He twisted and looked up at the hillside, where a plume of dust was beginning to rise. Instantly, he realized what was going on and knew that they were all in deadly danger.

"Avalanche!" he shouted at Sandy as he wheeled the Ovaro around. "Avalanche!"

The coach was about a hundred yards behind him. Sandy had heard the rumble and knew what it meant, too. The trail was too narrow for the coach to turn around, at least not without taking a lot of time to do it. Sandy's only option was to whip up the horses to their top speed and try to outrace the rocks now tumbling down the face of the hill toward the trail.

If he failed, the avalanche would sweep the coach right off the top of the cliff into the ocean. No one on board would survive the fall.

Fargo watched, every muscle in his body tense, as Sandy sent the coach careening along the narrow trail. A single misstep by one of the horses would pile up the team, and that would probably result in the coach going over the edge, too. Behind the racing vehicle came Jimmy with the lead rope attached to the extra horses gripped in his hand. He couldn't get past the coach on the trail so he followed it.

Fargo didn't think the youngster would abandon Angie anyway, even if it had been possible. The girl was inside the coach with Belinda and Grayson. By now they had to have realized what was going on, and they were probably terrified. They were trapped there, unable to do anything to save their own lives.

The rumble had turned into a roar, and the plume of dust was now a rolling cloud. Fargo saw trees snap and go down under the power of the avalanche. The stagecoach seemed to be traveling in slow motion as it came toward Fargo with the rockslide closing in from above.

A small rock about the size of a carpetbag bounded

through the air and struck the roof of the coach a glancing blow. It bounced off and kept going. That was the vanguard of the avalanche. That was how close it came to destroying the vehicle.

Then the rest of the hellish storm of stone swept on past, mere yards behind the stagecoach.

"Jimmy," Fargo grated. He couldn't see past the coach because of the boiling dust cloud, but Jimmy had been behind it, and now there was nothing back there but the avalanche.

Sandy's bearded face was ashen under its tan as the jehu brought the coach to a rocking, swaying halt a few yards short of where Fargo sat on the stallion. As soon as the coach stopped, one of the doors flew open and Angie leaped out. "Jimmy!" she shrieked as she stared back at the destruction behind them. "Oh, God, Jimmy!"

The roar was dying away now as the avalanche lost force. The trail was blocked by tons of rock that would take a week or more to clear away. Angie looked at it and wailed, "Jimmy!"

A tentative voice came from the back of the coach. "Y-yeah, Angie?"

She had covered her face with her hands as wretched sobs racked her body, but she stopped and jerked her head up as she heard those words. Fargo was surprised, too, but a grin spread over his face as Jimmy's head rose above the roof of the coach at the back of the vehicle. He was clinging to the rear boot, and Fargo guessed that he must have leaped from his horse onto the back of the stage when he saw that he wasn't going to be able to avoid the crushing rocks any other way.

"Jimmy!" Angie cried again, but this time her voice was filled with joy. As the young man dropped to the ground, she ran to him and threw herself into his arms. She said, "Jimmy, I thought you were dead!"

"No, but I sure didn't miss it by much," he said as he embraced her and gave her an awkward pat on the back. His eyes widened in shock as she lifted her head and pressed her mouth to his in a passionate kiss.

Belinda and Grayson climbed out of the coach and smiled at the reunion going on. Grayson's smile vanished, though, as he looked back down the trail and surveyed the damage done by the avalanche.

"What about the other horses?" he asked.

"Gone, I reckon," Fargo said. "One more thing Stoddard has to answer for. But losing them won't keep us from getting to San Francisco. The team that's already hitched up can take us the rest of the way if it has to."

Grayson nodded. "Yes, you're right. And blocking the trail like that won't have any effect on the stagecoach line, either, since it won't run through here on a regular basis. Stoddard has failed again."

"And I reckon he knows that by now," Fargo said. "All that dust will have hidden us from his men for a while, but enough of it has blown away by now so that they must have seen we're still alive. We'd better get moving before—"

Too late, he realized a second later as a rifle blasted and a bullet tore through the air next to his ear.

They were already under attack again.

13

"Everybody behind the coach!" Fargo shouted as he threw himself out of the saddle. He slapped the Ovaro on the rump and sent the stallion galloping along the trail, out of the line of fire.

Given their situation, trying to flee would do no good. The riflemen hidden in the trees on the slope above them would be able to pick them off one by one, because the coach couldn't go very fast on this narrow, twisting trail.

Anyway, even if they had tried to escape, the first one the bushwhackers shot would be Sandy, halting the stagecoach again.

Fargo brought the Sharps to his shoulder and fired at a puff of powder smoke he spotted on the hillside. He didn't know if he hit anything, but at least he was putting up a fight. Meanwhile, the other five people scrambled behind the big Concord coach. More shots came from the slope, and bullets thudded into the vehicle.

Fargo ducked behind the team and moved in a crouching run toward the coach. As he did, he heard the meaty sound of lead striking flesh behind him, and one of the horses screamed in pain. A bitter taste filled Fargo's mouth as he realized that the gunmen planned to kill all the members of the team. That would strand the stagecoach here and accomplish Hiram Stoddard's goal of preventing it from reaching San Francisco.

Fargo drew his Colt and sprayed the hillside with slugs, hoping that would force Stoddard's men to hunt some cover, and buy him and his companions a few minutes. From behind the coach, Sandy and Jimmy opened up with their guns as well.

Reaching the coach, Fargo pressed the Sharps into Grayson's hands. "You still have cartridges for it?" he asked.

Grayson nodded. "Thanks, Skye. One good shot at those bastards is all I want."

"Maybe I can flush them out for you," Fargo said as he thumbed fresh rounds into his Colt. He snapped the cylinder of the big revolver closed. "I'm going to take the fight to them."

"Skye, what are you—" Belinda began, but before she could finish the question, he had tossed his hat aside, left the cover of the coach, and sprinted for the trees, moving at an angle and darting back and forth to make himself a more difficult target to hit.

Bullets whined around his head and smacked into the rocky ground around his feet. But he managed to reach the trees without being hit, and once he was among the pines, he knew the bushwhackers couldn't see him anymore. Like a wolf among sheep, he launched into a deadly game of hunter and hunted— although these "sheep" were heavily armed and just as capable of killing him as he was of killing them.

Fargo moved through the woods and up the slope with a stealth that was second nature to him, as silent and swift as a Comanche. He holstered the Colt and drew the Arkansas toothpick instead. At close quarters, the long, heavy knife was a terrible weapon.

The firing died away, and he heard a low-voiced call. "Damn it, where's Fargo? I'm not worried about any of those other pilgrims."

"He made it into the trees," another man replied. His voice held an edge of fear. "He's probably up here among us by now."

"All right, kill the damn horses and let's get out of here," the first man said. Fargo recognized the voice. It belonged to the hardcase called Elam, who must have recovered at least somewhat from the wound Fargo had given him in Los Angeles.

Elam was farther away, but the man who had answered him was close by, no more than a dozen feet from Fargo. Not making a sound, Fargo closed in on him. The man crouched behind a thick-trunked pine tree. He was drawing a bead on the stagecoach team with his rifle when Fargo's left arm looped around his neck and jerked him upright.

Fargo could have cut his throat and killed him with little or no sound, but instead he thrust the blade into the bushwhacker's back and loosened his hold on the man's neck so that a scream of agony ripped from his throat. The shriek echoed across the hillside.

The gunmen had started to open fire again, but only a couple of shots had sounded before they heard the scream and stopped pulling their triggers. "What the hell was that?" one man yelled, giving away his position.

Fargo pulled the toothpick free and let the bushwhacker's limp body fall to the ground.

"It's Fargo! Fargo must've gotten one of us!"

A grim smile touched Fargo's mouth. That was what he wanted to hear. He wanted them spooked. It would make them careless.

He cat-footed through the trees toward another of

the men and came upon him kneeling behind a bush. The man heard the rustle of pine needles under Fargo's booted feet and whirled around with a startled shout, trying to bring his rifle to bear as he did so.

Fargo's left hand closed around the rifle barrel and wrenched the weapon aside, while at the same time his right drove the toothpick into the bushwhacker's belly. The hombre screeched in pain, but the scream trailed off into a gurgle as Fargo ripped upward with the blade, opening him up and spilling his guts out. Fargo shoved the dying man away from him.

Killing so brutally went against the grain for the Trailsman, but he was facing long odds. And he knew that none of these men would hesitate to kill the folks who had taken cover behind the stagecoach. They were hired guns and more than likely had blood on their hands from way back.

The second scream was still echoing when a man shouted, "Damn it, Elam, I'm gettin' out of here!"

"Me, too!" called another man. "I'm not gonna sit here and wait for Fargo to kill me!"

"You sorry bastards!" Elam bellowed. "Come back here and finish the job!"

His companions must have been more afraid of Fargo than they were of him, however, because a moment later, when the shooting started again, only one rifle spoke. Fargo felt confident that it belonged to Elam.

One might be enough, though, unless Fargo could silence it in a hurry. Another horse in the stagecoach team gave a shrill whinny of pain as a bullet struck it.

Fargo forgot about being quiet. He stuck the Arkansas toothpick back in its sheath, drew his Colt, and crashed through the brush toward the sound of the shots. Elam must have heard him coming because the big hardcase was already turning toward Fargo as the Trailsman burst into a tiny clearing where Elam was crouched behind a screen of trees.

The rifle in the man's hands blasted as Fargo threw himself forward. The slug whistled over Fargo's head. He squeezed off a shot as he hit the ground, aiming at Elam's chest. Elam moved just as Fargo pulled the trigger, though, and the bullet dug a shallow furrow in his upper right arm instead.

That was enough to make Elam yell in pain and drop his rifle. Rather than try to recover it, he flung himself backward, behind the shelter of the trees. Fargo's second shot knocked some bark off the rough trunk of a pine, but that was all the damage it did.

Biting back a curse, Fargo leaped to his feet as he heard Elam heading down the slope toward the trail. The man might have dropped his rifle, but he still had a handgun, and he still represented a threat to Belinda, Grayson, and the others.

Fargo went after him.

"Watch out down there!" he shouted to those who had remained with the coach. "Elam's headed your way!"

As Fargo raced through the woods, he caught glimpses of Elam but never got a good enough look to take a shot. Also, he ran the risk that, if he missed, his bullet might range on down the slope and out of the trees, where it could hit one of his friends. Grimacing, he holstered the Colt.

He caught up with Elam just as the hardcase reached the edge of the trees. Fargo threw himself at the man in a diving tackle. He caught Elam around the knees and brought him down. Elam twisted and slashed at Fargo's head with the barrel of his gun, which he held in his left hand now because his right arm was wounded.

Fargo jerked his head aside so that the blow missed, but the gun thudded into his shoulder and sent knives of pain stabbing through his arm before the limb went numb. Fargo reached across his body and grabbed Elam's left wrist with his left hand. Wrestling like that was awkward for both men, but Fargo managed to hold the gun off so that Elam couldn't bring the barrel in line for a shot.

Fargo brought his knee up and slammed it into Elam's midsection. Elam grunted at the impact but didn't stop fighting. His right arm was wounded, but unlike Fargo, he could still use it. He grappled with Fargo and got his right hand on the Trailsman's neck. The fingers clamped down in a cruel grip that cut off Fargo's air.

Knowing that he couldn't last long like that, Fargo used his feet, kicking hard against the ground so that both he and Elam rolled over and started to topple down the slope. Brush tore at them but didn't stop them. They emerged from the trees and went over the edge of a rocky outcropping. With nothing but air under them, Fargo felt himself falling.

He didn't know how long the drop was going to be. It was only about five feet, but that was enough for the hard landing to knock him and Elam apart. Some of the feeling was coming back into Fargo's right arm. He reached for the Arkansas toothpick.

But Elam had been able to hang on to his gun, and now, a few feet away from Fargo, the big hardcase was swinging the weapon up. Fargo knew he wouldn't be able to reach his knife in time. Elam grinned as he prepared to splatter the Trailsman's brains all over the hillside.

Three shots roared so close together that they sounded like one giant explosion. Slugs from the handguns fired by Sandy and Jimmy smacked into

Elam's back. It was doubtful that he ever felt the bullets' impact, though, because at the same time a .52 caliber round fired by Arthur Grayson from Fargo's Sharps struck him in the back of the head.

Fargo winced and turned his face aside from the crimson destruction. Elam's body flopped forward, most of its head gone. The revolver slipped unfired from the hardcase's fingers.

Fargo pushed himself to his feet and stepped past the corpse. As the echoes of the volley rolled away, the hillside became silent except for the never-ending sound of the sea at the base of the cliffs. The three men emerged from the shelter of the coach, but Grayson told Belinda and Angie to stay put for the moment.

"Fargo, are you all right?" Sandy asked as Fargo came up to the stagecoach.

Flexing the fingers of his right hand as feeling fully returned to it, Fargo nodded. "Yes, I'm fine, thanks to you fellas. That was good shooting."

"Are the rest of them gone?" Grayson asked.

Fargo nodded. "Except for the ones I killed. The others spooked and lit a shuck. Anybody hurt down here?"

Sandy spat and said in disgust, "Only a couple o' the horses. They're dead. I hope them sumbitches who shot 'em burn in hell. I never did hold with hurtin' animals."

"The other horses are all right?"

Jimmy was checking them as Fargo asked the question. The young man turned and said, "One of 'em's got a bullet crease on his rump, but it don't amount to much. They can all travel."

"Then we've still got a four-horse hitch," Grayson said. "That will be slower, but they can still pull the coach."

Fargo nodded. It would take a while to unhitch the

two dead horses and rearrange the team, but even though the avalanche and the ambush had slowed them down, it wasn't going to stop them.

"Let's get to work," he said.

The sun was past its zenith by the time the stagecoach was rolling again. The grisly task of unhitching the two dead horses and toppling them off the edge of the trail to plummet to the rocks below had taken quite a while, just as Fargo had predicted. He hoped they would be able to put their hands on some fresh horses when they reached the town of Santa Cruz, just the other side of Monterey Bay.

That proved to be the case. The old Spanish settlement near the mission had several livery stables. Grayson found some suitable draft animals at one of them, and although he had to pay a steep price for them, the proprietor having figured out that Grayson was over a barrel, not long past the middle of the afternoon the stagecoach was on the trail again, being pulled by the fresh team of six horses.

A decent road ran between Santa Cruz and San Francisco, through hills that were covered with giant redwood trees. Fargo had seen those towering old-timers before, but they never failed to impress him.

Not that there was much time to take in the scenery. Sandy was driving the team for all it was worth, taking the bends in the trail at a clip that was a little faster than it might have been under other circumstances. Everyone wanted to reach San Francisco as soon as possible, though, because once the coach rolled into the city by the bay, Hiram Stoddard would no longer have any reason to harm them. He would have failed in his quest to stop Arthur Grayson's stagecoach from reaching San Francisco first.

Fargo rode about fifty yards in front of the coach.

He no longer needed to range as far ahead as he had earlier in the trip. Now he was more guard than guide, keeping his eyes open for any last-ditch ambush attempt by Stoddard's men.

Stoddard might not *have* any men anymore, Fargo mused. Since Elam was dead, along with two more of the bushwhackers who had struck on the trail alongside Monterey Bay, the rest of the hired guns might have decided that enough was enough. The only loyalty hardcases like that had was to money, and they valued their lives more than they did anything else.

From the hills covered with redwood trees, the trail dropped into the broad Santa Clara Valley, then rose again into the hills at the southern end of the peninsula that ran between the Pacific Ocean and San Francisco Bay. The bustling, cosmopolitan city of San Francisco, once a sleepy Spanish village called Yerba Buena, sat at the northern tip of the peninsula. In the ten years since the discovery of gold in California, the city had exploded in size and population. It had endured some growing pains along the way. The violence and vice that had plagued the areas known as Portsmouth Square and the Barbary Coast had led to the rise of Committees of Vigilance that had cleaned out the more unsavory elements.

Portsmouth Square and the Barbary Coast were still there, and the establishments that called them home still did a brisk business in gambling and whoring, but things had settled down enough by now that the vigilantes, as they were called, had disbanded. Fargo had several favorite saloons along the Barbary Coast and was looking forward to visiting them. After the long, dangerous trip from Los Angeles, some good whiskey and maybe a friendly poker game would be excellent diversions.

The reddish-gold orb of the sun had lowered itself

into the Pacific by the time the stagecoach rolled through all the smaller villages south of San Francisco. Dusk was beginning to cloak the countryside as the vehicle climbed up one last hill. Fargo reined in at the top of that rise and lifted a hand to Sandy, signaling for him to stop. The jehu called out to his team as he hauled back on the lines. As the coach rocked to a halt, Arthur Grayson called from inside, "What's wrong, Skye? Why have we stopped?"

"Thought you might like to get out and take a look around," Fargo said as he swung down from the saddle.

The coach door opened and Grayson climbed out, followed by Belinda and Angie. Jimmy was riding on the driver's seat with Sandy, so he had already seen what Fargo was talking about. He dropped to the ground and stood next to Angie, slipping an arm around her shoulders as he did so.

From here, the travelers gazed out over the city. It was already dark enough so that the lights of San Francisco glittered brightly as they spread across the end of the peninsula. To the right was the bay, to the left the Pacific Ocean itself, lit by the fading glow of the sun. Northward, across the opening between ocean and bay known as the Golden Gate, lay wooded hills that stretched on up the coast all the way to Oregon Territory.

"There it is," Fargo told them. "San Francisco."

The ocean breeze was refreshing, and they stood there in silence for a long moment, embracing the wind, awed by the sight before them.

"Oh, Skye," Belinda finally said as she placed a hand on his arm and leaned against his shoulder. "It's beautiful."

"It certainly is," Grayson agreed. "A part of me can't believe we're finally here."

"We ain't all the way there yet," Sandy pointed out. "We still got a little ways to go."

Fargo said, "Sandy's right. We'd better get moving. I'd hate to get this close and then have Stoddard stop us."

Even as he spoke, he halfway expected somebody to take a shot at them again. But the beautiful evening remained quiet and peaceful, and a short time later, the stagecoach rolled onto the cobblestone streets of San Francisco.

The journey was over.

14

Before ever coming west, Arthur Grayson had written a letter to the Metropole Hotel, the finest in San Francisco, reserving rooms for him and his daughter upon their arrival. That was where Fargo found himself later that evening, having dinner in a luxuriously furnished dining room lit by sparkling crystal chandeliers.

Even though he wore clean buckskins, he knew he looked out of place in such fancy surroundings, and the waiters who worked in the hotel dining room made no secret of the fact that *they* thought he didn't belong there. But Fargo had never been the sort of man to let such things bother him. He was comfortable just being himself, no matter where he was or who he was with.

Tonight he was with Belinda Grayson, who looked lovely in a dark blue, low-cut gown as she sat across from him. Her father had dined with her and Fargo, but he had gone on up to his room, leaving the two of them alone. Grayson had meetings lined up the next day with the most prominent businessmen and bankers in San Francisco, to discuss his new stagecoach line with them, and he wanted to be well rested. Fargo wasn't sure where Jimmy and Angie were, but he would have been willing to bet money that they were together, wherever they were.

Sandy had headed for the nearest saloon, vowing to get drunk and stay drunk for a week. Fargo didn't doubt that he could manage that.

Fargo and Belinda had lingered over snifters of brandy after dinner. She smiled at him now over hers and said, "I'm ready to go upstairs. How about you, Skye?"

Fargo yawned, making a show of covering his mouth with his hand, and said, "Yeah, I'm pretty tired, all right. Looking forward to a good night's sleep for a change. Nothing but some nice, undisturbed sleep."

"Keep that up and that's *all* you'll get," Belinda scolded, but the smile on her face took any sting out of her words. Fargo knew that she was anticipating what the evening would bring as much as he was. Once again they would join in making love, a merging of body and passion that would send both of them to the heights of pleasure. Fargo lifted his glass and clinked it against hers, then drained what was left of the brandy.

A smile with a trace of sadness in it touched Belinda's beautiful face. "I suppose now that we've reached the end of the trail, so to speak, you'll be moving on, Skye?"

"Not right away," Fargo assured her. "I'd like to take a few days to let my horse rest, stock up on supplies, things like that." He inclined his head. "But the time will come when I'll be riding. I won't lie to you about that, or anything else, Belinda. I'm a long way from being ready to settle down."

"I know that," she said with a hint of wistfulness in her voice. "But a girl can dream, can't she?"

"Everybody can dream," Fargo said. "This old world would be a pretty sad place without them."

A few minutes later, arm in arm, they climbed the opulent staircase and went down the second-floor hallway toward Belinda's room. Fargo felt his pulse quickening as he thought about how they would soon be nude together in a big, comfortable bed, with the whole night in front of them to do delicious things to and with each other.

When they reached the door, Belinda handed him the key to the room. He unlocked the door and went in first, taking a match from his pocket to light the lamp.

Before he could strike the lucifer, something crashed into the back of his head. It felt like the whole world had fallen in on him, and as he plummeted into darkness, Fargo realized that even though Hiram Stoddard had been defeated, he had one thing still driving him on.

Vengeance.

"Mr. Fargo! Skye!"

Fargo heard the voice and felt a hand shaking his shoulder. He climbed back up out of the black morass that had claimed him. A shake of his head cleared away the cobwebs, and he knew right away what had happened. Either Stoddard or someone working for him had found out which room was Belinda's, and they had been waiting there for her. But Fargo had come in first, and the lurker had knocked him out.

He wasn't surprised to see Arthur Grayson kneeling beside him with a frightened look on his face. Fargo shoved himself to his feet and said, "What's happened? Where's Belinda?"

"They took her," Grayson said in a voice ragged with terror.

"Stoddard's men?"

Grayson jerked his head in a nod. "It must have

been. A note was delivered to my room a few minutes ago saying that if I want to see Belinda alive again, I have to abandon my plans for the stagecoach line. If I agree to do that, I'm supposed to come to some place on the Barbary Coast called Red Mike's, and Belinda will be returned safely to me there."

Fargo shook his head, even though that made it throb with pain. "It's a trap," he said. "Stoddard's just trying to lure you down there so he can kill you. And then he'll go right ahead with whatever he has in mind for Belinda."

"I—I was afraid that was his plan. But what else can I do? The note said that if I went to the authorities, Belinda would be killed."

"I reckon you'll have to go to this Red Mike's. But you won't be going alone."

Before Fargo could say anything else, hurrying footsteps sounded in the hall. Jimmy appeared in the open door, saying, "Mr. Fargo! Something terrible's happened!"

Fargo and Grayson turned to him. "They got Angie, too?" Fargo asked.

"Yeah." Jimmy blinked in confusion. He had a bloody gash on his forehead where something had struck him, probably a pistol. "What do you mean? Where's Miss Belinda?"

"Stoddard has her, along with Angie," Fargo replied. "And we're going to get both of them back. Do you know where Sandy went?"

"He said somethin' about a place called the Pirate's Den. I reckon it must be a tavern."

"Find out where it is," Fargo said, "and find Sandy. He'll know where Red Mike's is. That's where Mr. Grayson and I are headed. You and Sandy get there as soon as you can. Can you remember that?"

Jimmy's head bobbed up and down. "You bet I can.

I know I ain't the smartest fella in the world, but with Angie's life at stake, I won't forget what you told me."

"I know you won't." Fargo clapped a hand on Jimmy's shoulder as he and Grayson left the room. "Good man. Don't waste any time."

"I sure won't." Jimmy turned and ran down the hall toward the stairs.

Fargo turned to Grayson. "You have a pistol?"

"In my valise."

"Get it. I'll meet you downstairs."

A couple of minutes later, Fargo and Grayson left the Metropole and strode toward the area known as the Barbary Coast. Even though it had calmed down somewhat from its heyday, it was still a dangerous place, and Fargo figured that before the night was over it would once again see more than its share of death.

The usual fog had rolled in, throwing a wet cloak over the city. A scandalized desk clerk at the hotel had told Fargo where Red Mike's was located, but warned the two men to stay away from there. It was a notorious dive, the scene of many murders over the years. Fargo and Grayson ignored the warning, of course.

When they reached their destination, Fargo saw a dim light burning over the doorway of the squat, two-story frame building only a block from the waterfront. He pointed it out to Grayson and said, "Give me a couple of minutes and then go on inside."

"What are you going to do?"

"I'll see if I can get in the back."

"Stoddard will have guards posted," Grayson cautioned.

"Then I'll just have to be quieter than they are," Fargo said.

He left Grayson there and circled the block to approach the back of Red Mike's along a narrow, stinking alley so dark that Fargo had to make his way as much by instinct as anything. He gripped the Arkansas toothpick, not wanting to alert anyone inside with a shot. With his other hand he felt along the wall, searching for a door. Even back here, the fog had penetrated and made it more difficult to see.

His hand touched the wood of a door at the same time as someone bumped into him in the darkness. The man muttered a curse. Fargo sensed as much as heard something sweeping through the air toward his head. He ducked, and an instant later heard a club of some sort miss his skull by inches. He brought the big knife up and felt the blade bite deep into flesh.

He managed to close his other hand around the guard's neck before the man could let out a yell. Fargo pushed the toothpick deeper and then ripped it free. The guard collapsed. Fargo let him slump to the filthy floor of the alley.

A groan tried to well up in Fargo's throat as he tried the door and found it barred on the inside. He knew he wouldn't be able to break it down. But as he tilted his head back and looked up into the darkness, he wondered if Stoddard would have thought to have the windows on the second floor fastened as well.

Fargo sheathed the Arkansas toothpick and began running his hands over the rough planks of the wall, finding tiny gaps and imperfections to serve as handholds. He pulled himself up, grunting with the effort required to hang on and climb the almost sheer wall. Working his way along it by feel, he found a window and tried it. The pane slid up.

Fargo slipped inside, hoping that he wouldn't find himself in the room of some whore who would scream because he had disturbed her at her work. The room seemed to be empty, though. Fargo crossed to the door and eased it open. He heard angry voices from down below as he stepped out onto a narrow balcony that overlooked the tavern's main room.

The light from the lamps didn't penetrate very far into the smoky air up here. Shadows wrapped Fargo as he drew his Colt and edged toward the balcony's railing. He looked down and saw Arthur Grayson standing not far inside the door of the tavern. Grayson was scared, but he was mad and determined, too, as he faced Hiram Stoddard and a couple of hardcases, probably the only ones left from Stoddard's gang of hired guns. Off to one side, behind a bar, stood a tall, burly man with a shock of red hair and a red mustache. That would be Mike, the proprietor of the place, Fargo thought. Stoddard must have paid him to run everybody off and close down for the night, because there were no customers.

One other man stood in front of the bar, though, and his presence came as a surprise to Fargo. Matthias Jarlberg had his left hand wrapped around Angie's right arm, while on his other side, he gripped Belinda's left arm with his right hand. He had followed them from Los Olivos, as Fargo had thought that he might, looking for Angie and revenge. Somehow, he had joined forces with Hiram Stoddard.

"—should have known better than to cross me again, Grayson," Stoddard was saying. "You've brought this on yourself."

"Do what you want to me," Grayson said, "but let Belinda and that other poor girl go. They haven't done anything to you."

Stoddard chuckled. "Unfortunately, I can't do that. You see, once I ran into Mr. Jarlberg here and realized that we had the same goal, I had to promise he could take the young lady back with him and do whatever he wanted to her if he would help me. And your charming daughter is to be the payment for my new friend Mike. There's no need for you to worry yourself about what's going to happen to her, though. You'll be dead and won't be able to worry about anything."

"Fargo's going to hunt you down and kill you," Grayson said. "You know that, don't you? No matter what you do to us, you're a dead man."

Now there was irritation in Stoddard's voice as he snapped, "Yes, well, I wish I had known that my men were going to cross paths with Mr. Fargo tonight. If I had, I would have given them specific orders to go ahead and kill him while he was unconscious. As it was, they thought it was more important to bring Miss Grayson back here to me right away."

So that was why he was still alive, Fargo thought. A stroke of luck . . . but he would take it.

"You're sure Grayson's body will never be found?" Stoddard said to the redheaded bruiser behind the bar.

"Not a chance," Mike rumbled. "The bay keeps its secrets."

"Very well, then. Let's get this over with."

That sounded good to Fargo. He called out, "That's right. Let's end this."

And with that, he put his free hand on the balcony railing and vaulted over it.

He had already picked out the open space on the floor where he intended to land. The Colt in his hand was roaring and bucking even as he dropped through the air. One of Stoddard's men doubled over and collapsed as the Trailsman's bullets ripped into his belly. The other dropped his gun and staggered back, pressing his hands to the wounds in his chest as blood welled from them.

Stoddard screamed a frustrated curse as he clawed a pistol from under his coat. He fired at Fargo, forgetting Grayson for a second. That was a mistake, because Grayson had his gun out and blazed away with it, aiming across the room at Stoddard. Gasping in surprise and pain, Stoddard reeled back and looked down at the crimson blooming on his vest and fancy white shirt.

Fargo landed cleanly, rolled to break his fall, and came up ready to fire again. He didn't get a chance to, because Jarlberg had flung the two young women aside and lifted one of the tavern's small round tables. He lunged at Fargo, roaring in rage as he smashed the table into the Trailsman. Fargo went over backward under the impact, which also knocked the Colt out of his hand. The table had shattered, leaving Jarlberg gripping a leg of it in each hand. He lifted them, clearly intending to use them to smash Fargo's brains out.

That was when Jimmy and Sandy came in the door. The revolver in Jimmy's hand spat flame as he emptied it into Jarlberg's massive body. Even as big and strong as Jarlberg was, the smashing impact of the slugs drove him backward in a grisly dance. The table legs slipped from his hands and he sat down hard, winding up with his back propped against the bar. He gasped, shuddered, and died.

At the same time, Red Mike lifted a scattergun from under the bar and swung it toward Sandy, but the rifle in the jehu's hands spoke first. The bullet took Mike in the face and threw him backward. He bounced off the backbar and pitched forward to hang over the bar itself, his arms dangling limply in death.

Sandy lowered the rifle and announced, "That's damn fine shootin' for a man who's drunk as a skunk, I'd say." He looked over at Grayson and added, "Told you I was better drunk than sober."

Grayson wasn't paying attention. He was too busy hugging his daughter and sobbing in relief that she was still alive.

Jimmy ran over to Angie, picked her up from the floor where she had fallen when Jarlberg shoved her away, and cradled her in his arms. She kept telling him that she was all right, but he didn't seem to believe her. He had to keep stroking her hair and kissing her to make sure.

Fargo picked himself up, retrieved his Colt, and reloaded it. He checked on Stoddard and the two hired guns. All of them were dead. Grayson was going to have a lot of explaining to do to the law. Even for San Francisco, this was a damned bloody mess and one hell of a way to conduct business. But Fargo had no doubt that Grayson would be able to make the authorities see that the killings had been justified.

That was one bad thing about civilization, Fargo mused. You couldn't always just stamp the snakes that needed stamping and be done with it.

Sandy went to the bar with his rifle canted over his shoulder and picked up a bottle of whiskey that was sitting there. He pulled the cork with his teeth, spit it out, and said, "Gonna be lots o' cryin' and carryin' on for a while. Reckon I'll have another drink."

"I think I'll join you," Fargo said. He was already looking forward to getting back to the wild lonesome, back to the frontier that would always be his home.

LOOKING FORWARD!

**The following is the opening
section of the next novel in the exciting
Trailsman series from Signet:**

THE TRAILSMAN #310
ALASKAN VENGEANCE

*Alaska, 1861—where old hatreds snare the
unwary in a web of deceit and bloodshed.*

Skye Fargo wished he was sober. He had not been
drunk in a coon's age. It had been so long, he had
almost forgotten what it felt like, which was just as
well, because he felt like hell. His head was pounding
to the beat of an invisible hammer, and his stomach
was threatening to bring up all the coffin varnish he
had chugged, plus his supper, besides. As if that were
not enough, his eyes kept going out of focus. The saloon, and everyone and everything in it, would be

blurry for a while, then his vision would clear again. It was a calamity in the making.

Fargo was pretty sure he had the best hand. A full house was usually a winner. He especially liked that he had three aces and two queens since that meant the other players had that many fewer high cards. But should he go whole hog and bet all the money he had won over the past couple of hours, or should he bow out? He had asked himself the question several times, and in his befuddled state, he could not decide.

"Hell of a note," Fargo muttered as he struggled to whip his sluggish brain into working as it should.

"What was that, friend?" asked the drummer on his left. The man oozed an oily charm that fooled no one.

Two of the other three players were big, brawny timbermen. They only bet when they had good hands and were misers with their chips.

The last player was a puzzlement. He wore a new suit and bowler hat and polished brown leather boots, but he was unshaven. He looked like a frontier rowdy but comported himself like a gentleman.

Of them all, only Fargo wore the garb of a true frontiersman: buckskins, boots, spurs, and a red bandanna. His white hat was brown with dust. It had taken him weeks to reach Seattle. He came in answer to a letter that had been waiting for him at Fort Laramie. The man who wrote the letter had wanted to hire the best scout alive—the man's exact words—to find his missing daughter. But when Fargo arrived in Seattle, he found out the missing daughter had in fact run off with a patent medicine salesman, and the man who had offered to hire him no longer needed to.

Fargo was not happy. He had come a long way at his own expense. The man offered to pay him twenty dollars for his troubles, but since Fargo had spent twice that on supplies and ammunition and a new bridle for his pinto, he almost threw the twenty dollars at the man's feet. Necessity overrode his pride, and Fargo used the twenty to buy not one but two bottles of red-eye, and chips so he could sit in on the poker game.

That had been hours ago. Now the bottles were empty and Fargo's head was pounding and he was nearly a thousand dollars richer than he had been when he walked in. He was having an incredible string of luck. The kind most only experienced once or twice in their lifetimes. The kind where the cards not only favored a man, they adored him.

The other players were not happy. They were staring at Fargo as if he were a snake they had found in their midst.

"It is your turn to bet, mister," one of the lumberjacks said.

"Oh, hell," Fargo said. He was tired of wrestling with the liquor. "I might as well go whole hog." He pushed every chip he had to the middle of the table.

The drummer let out an exaggerated sigh and set his cards down. "I regret I must fold. The cards have not been kind to me tonight."

"They have been kind to him," the second lumberman said resentfully, jabbing a thick finger at Fargo.

"Downright amazing how kind they have been," echoed the first. "It's almost enough to make me think he has them trained to do what he wants."

The drummer stiffened. "Now, now. Let's not have that kind of talk, shall we? I have been watching him closely and I can assure you he has not been cheating."

"No, he has not," said the man in the bowler. He

had a thick mustache laced with gray. "He has been most careful when it has been his turn to deal."

"I know," the timberman reluctantly agreed, his mouth curling in a lopsided grin. "I almost wish he was cheating, though, so I could get my money back."

Fargo smiled. "I have a wish of my own. I wish I was playing millionaires."

The others laughed, and the drummer said, "You are not doing too bad, friend. The pot is close to four thousand."

All eyes swung to the man in the bowler. It was his turn to bet. He stared at the pile of chips, then at his cards, then chewed on his lower lip before saying, "I do not have enough to stay in but I do not care to fold. Would it be all right if I bet something of equal or greater value?"

"Cash or coin," one of the timbermen said gruffly.

"We agreed on that at the start," said the second.

"Indeed we did," the man in the bowler replied. "But since the rest of you have bowed out, maybe we should let the gentleman in buckskins decide."

"I don't need a watch," Fargo said, alluding to the gold fob visible on the man's vest.

The man chuckled and shook his head. "I wouldn't part with it in any event. No, I was talking about something else." He reached inside his jacket and drew out a long, slender wallet. From it he took a folded sheet of paper.

"What's that?" the drummer asked.

"This," the man said as he unfolded it, "happens to be a legal document. It is a claim to my gold mine."

Fargo was drunk but he was not *that* drunk. "What are you trying to pull?" Passing off fake claims was a favorite tactic of swindlers.

"My name is Frank Toomey," the man said. "I have just come from Alaska. My mine, the Susie T, has been duly filed on and recorded. I would like to wager the claim."

Fargo's head was pounding worse than ever. It did not help that the saloon was thick with cigar smoke and the reek of unwashed bodies. Lowering his hand under the table, he slowly drew his Colt and just as slowly placed it on the table.

Frank Toomey's eyebrows tried to come together above his nose. "What is that for?"

"For jackasses who think I am one and try to cheat me," Fargo bluntly answered.

Toomey set his cards facedown and spread his hands in front of him. "I assure you I am not trying to cheat you. The mine exists. My claim is in order. Win the pot and the Susie T is yours."

"Listen to yourself," Fargo said in disgust. "You want me to believe that you'll risk losing a gold mine for a pot this size?" In high-stakes games it was not unusual to have pots worth hundreds of thousands. Compared to that kind of money, four thousand was paltry.

"Hear me out, if you would be so kind," Frank Toomey urged. "Yes, I have a gold mine. But that does not mean I have a lot of money. I only recently filed, and I need equipment and whatnot to get the mine up and running. In fact, that is why I came to Seattle. To scrounge up the capital I need to make the Susie T a going concern."

"How much gold have you brought out of the ground so far?" Fargo asked.

"Enough nuggets to fill the poke that I used to get to Seattle and to buy the chips to play at this table," Toomey replied.

"That's all?"

One of the lumberjacks snorted.

"So what you are saying," Fargo continued, "is that this gold mine of yours could be next to worthless?" He had seen it before. Ore hounds who thought they had struck the mother lode.

"I know what you are thinking. But I have seen the vein. I chipped the nuggets out myself. There is gold, and a lot of it." Toomey indicated the pot. "To you that might not seem like all that much, but four thousand will buy a lot of the things I need."

"I don't know," Fargo said.

"The equipment will be mine, free and clear," Toomey went on. "I won't have to pay it back, like the loan I hope to get at a bank. That's why I sat in, hoping to win a hand like this."

"You are taking an awful lot for granted."

"Maybe so," Toomey said. "Maybe betting the mine is a mistake. If so, it won't be my first, and probably not my last. So what do you say? Will you humor me? Let me wager the Susie T." He held the claim over the mound of chips.

"I must be loco," Fargo said, and nodded.

Frank Toomey made a show of neatly placing the folded paper on top. He picked up his cards. "I realize you go first but I can't wait, so if you will permit me." With a flourish he turned his cards over. "A full house," he announced. "Kings and twos."

"Not bad," Fargo acknowledged, "but not good enough." He showed his aces and queens.

Toomey had been about to reach for the pot. Disbelief marked his features—disbelief and something else. For a fleeting instant, anger registered—not the mild anger of a seasoned poker player who knew that losing was part of the game, but the intense, almost savage anger of someone who had a cherished prize snatched from their grasp.

"I tried to warn you," Fargo said.

Toomey had gone pale and gripped the edge of the table, as if afraid he would fall from his chair. "I was so sure."

Fargo raked in his winnings. He picked up the claim and, without unfolding it, said, "You need to sign this over to me."

"I don't have anything to write with," Frank Toomey said. "Perhaps you could stop by my room later. I'm staying at the Puget. Room thirteen." He took his pocket watch from his vest. "It is almost eight. I can meet you there in, say, an hour."

Fargo shrugged. It made no difference to him. "An hour it is." He stuffed the claim into a pocket and began to stack the chips so they would be easier to count.

One of the lumberjacks nudged the other. "Come on, Charlie. Let's belly up to the bar. I still have a few dollars left."

Their chairs scraped and they melted into the noisy throng that packed The Cork and Keg. The saloon was always crowded. Situated on the waterfront, it was a favorite haunt of residents, mariners and timbermen alike. The quality of the liquor had a lot to do with its popularity. So did the quality of the doves who mingled with the customers and encouraged them to buy more liquor. All were young, all were pretty, and all wore tight dresses that accented their shapely contours. Small wonder the saloon was also a favorite of Fargo's.

He was almost done stacking the chips when one of

those shapely figures materialized at his elbow. Enticing perfume made his nose tingle. A perfume he recognized. "Have a seat, Marie. I will be done in a minute."

Marie Davenport had curly black hair that fell in gorgeous ringlets past her slender shoulders. Her eyes were almost as black as her hair and gleamed with playful vitality. Her full lips were cherry red, her cheeks high and full, but nowhere near as full as the bosom that swelled her dress near to bursting at the seams. Her cleavage was the envy of every woman in the room. "Are you finally going to take me to supper as you promised?" she asked with a mock pout.

"I told you not to wait," Fargo said. "I told you the game could last half the night."

"I am lucky it didn't, then," Marie said, "because I am starved." She placed her warm hand on his arm and smiled ever so sweetly. "The restaurant I want to take you to has the thickest and juiciest steaks in all Seattle."

"And costs more than anywhere else, if I know you."

Marie's laugh tinkled on the air. "Can a girl help it if she has expensive tastes? Nice things do not come cheap."

"Steak sure doesn't," Fargo remarked. Not in Seattle. Timber was the main industry, not beef. The few cows to be had were owned by settlers who refused to part with their sole source of milk and cheese. So cattle for the restaurant trade had to be brought in on ships.

"Nearly everything costs more here," Marie mentioned. "But I don't mind. I make good money. And I like it here. I like the climate. I like the people."

"You like rain six months of the year?" Fargo teased.

"You're exaggerating. Yes, it rains a lot, but not that much, and no, I don't mind the rain or the clouds at all. Fact is, there is nothing I find more soothing and relaxing than a rainy day with the raindrops pattering on my roof and me curled up in a blanket. Unless maybe it is a hot bath."

"I can think of a third thing." Fargo smirked and stared at her pendulous breasts.

Giggling, Marie responded, "There is always that. But the relaxation comes after a lot of sweat and effort. A rainy day, a bath, they just are."

Fargo glanced up in genuine surprise. "Is that how you think of it? As sweat and effort?"

"Oh, no. I was using it as an example. It is fun. The most fun I know." Marie ran a long fingernail over the back of his hand, touching his skin ever so lightly. "I could not do without it."

Fargo made a show of wiping his brow with his sleeve. "That's a relief. For a second there you had me worried." He added the last chip to a stack. "Why don't you fetch your handbag and fluff your hair while I cash these in? Meet me out front in five minutes."

"Make it ten. Women must take their time when they fluff." Grinning, Marie squeezed his hand. "I can hardly wait for the fun."

Neither could Fargo. He was glad to step out in the fresh air. Lights sprinkled the green hills of Seattle like so many land-bound fireflies. It was hard to believe that not quite ten years ago Seattle had been an isolated outpost. Now it was a booming town with bright prospects thanks to the deep bay it bordered and the seagoing vessels that put in there. Stretching, he gazed out over the dark water and heard it lapping at the shore.

Suddenly something sharp pricked the small of his back and a gruff voice growled, "Don't move unless we say to, and don't let out a peep unless we say you can, and you might live out the night."

No other series packs this much heat!

THE TRAILSMAN

**Available wherever books are sold or at
penguin.com**

National Bestselling Author
RALPH COMPTON

Available wherever books are sold or at
penguin.com